MAGDALENA'S GHOST

THE HAUNTING OF THE HOUSE IN GALLOWS LANE

PEPPI HILTON

(Author of THE APPOINTMENT)

Copyright ©Peppi Hilton 2015

All rights reserved. No part of this publication may be reproduced, stored in a retrieval system, or transmitted in any form, or by any means, electronic, mechanical, photocopying, recording, or otherwise without the prior written permission of the author Peppi Hilton. The right of Peppi Hilton to be identified as the author of this work has been asserted by her in accordance with the Copyright Designs and Patents Act 1988

This book is a work of fiction and all the names and characters, unless quoted for the purpose of historical fact, have been created from the author's imagination and are purely fictional; and any resemblance to any persons, living or dead, or to any places other than geographical locations, or events, or incidents, is entirely coincidental.

ISBN-13: 978-1514188651
ISBN-10: 1514188651

Dedication to:

All those who fear the empty hours

And to my late brother Alan who once expressed an urge to write ghost stories when accompanying me on a visit to a mediaeval house. This is for him.

Contents

Prologue...1
1..9
2..23
3..26
4..36
5..42
6..53
7..71
8..75
9..84
10..102
11..120
12..133
13..156
14..168
15..180
Epilogue...191
Author's Note:..193

Prologue

She rocks alone in her old rocking chair
That little old lady with no-one to care
She lives with the memory of a youth she once had
Recapturing moments of the good and the bad
Years which have long since passed her by
And as she remembers a tear fills her eye
A little old lady who sits in the gloom
Of that cold dismal empty and sad lonely room
Slowly she rocks as each hour passes by
That little old lady just waiting to die

Peppi Hilton

BEFORE

THE TAXI-DRIVER PULLED INTO THE GROUNDS of the big old house as instructed. He looked up at the three-storey building and grimaced. He knew nothing about it, other than what his passenger had told him along the journey from her maisonette a couple of hundred miles away. It belonged to her elderly mother, she had told him without being prompted. She had decided to move into the property to take care of her, she had said, although the mother knew nothing about it. Wouldn't agree to it, she confessed. They didn't get on - never had. But it was going to belong to her one day, so might as well get used to living there again, was her opinion – and she voiced it strong. Glad to get away when she was younger; but now the old lady is showing signs of failing – so she'd heard along the grapevine – she's keen to move back in. He'd met her type before, many times. And then there was the cat. It had wailed all along the journey and he was not much pleased about that. But now he had finally arrived at the destination, thank God! The journey had been made monotonous by the constant drone of the woman's voice and her rat-bag harmonising in the background – not to mention the smell. He climbed out of the car, opened the boot and dragged out the suitcases, several of them. Goodness knows what's in them. By their weight he wouldn't be surprised if they contained all the family silver; although she didn't look as if she possessed anything worth a fortune. The clothes – for want of a better description – looked as if they'd come from the Salvation Army or a jumble sale. But on reflection, if they'd come from a jumble sale she'd have had to pay, and she didn't come across as someone who would part with her money easily. She admitted to renting the place she had left behind, and that didn't look up to much. But Juniper House, this was something else; landed on her feet by the look of it. This looked typical of the type of place that stood neglected while some old miser hid the money under the floorboards. Probably worth a fortune on the open market if someone did it up, although it wouldn't be for the faint-hearted he could tell that much. The daughter didn't sound like she had any intentions though; probably another one of them who hoards it and spends bugger-all! She had him beaten down on price for the journey up North, and he felt peeved about that. After all, if she could afford to travel by taxi in the first place she must have money stashed away somewhere. But times were hard and he couldn't afford to turn the job down. At least it would be a much pleasanter journey back.

She paid the fare, but left it short as she didn't have any loose change she said, and he didn't attempt to argue. He left her and the cat, which was still whining from its basket, at the entrance, a side door which was set back inside an old, open wooden porch, most of it beginning to rot. She rang the bell and he heard the chimes echo hollowly inside. He dropped the final case by her side and returned to his car. He climbed inside and drove off out of the grounds and back into Gallows Lane. He didn't bother to look back.

AFTER

THE WIND HOWLED through the loose window panes and the sound echoed along the empty corridors. Dust-ridden floorboards creaked and groaned, and the shadows of the night created images which danced on the bare walls as the moon seeped in through the gaps in the old wooden shutters. Outside, the leaves rustled as they were blown around the dense, overrun garden, and darkness cast eerie shadows across the tall gables of Juniper House. Inside, sounds could be heard in the distance, faint sounds of a piano playing a melancholy tune and a cat mewing as it mounted the stairs and wandered along the bare landings. An ageing woman was sound asleep in her bed, oblivious to any goings-on, that is until she heard a frail voice calling outside her bedroom door.

"Are we having a cup of tea?"

She sat bolt upright in bed, now wide-awake and listening. Everything was silent. But a few seconds later she heard the disturbing sound again, quite clearly this time: "Are we having a cup of tea?"

Her heart began to pump heavily as the fear ran through her veins, and she listened intently for the sound to repeat itself.

"Are we having a cup of tea?" echoed the faint, familiar sound which she recognised well.

"Mother, is that you?" her voice shaking as she spoke, not knowing whether to expect an answer or not.

But of course it couldn't be, and she couldn't answer – her mother was long dead.

She got out of bed nervously, her old bones bending with age as she hobbled over to the door. She hesitated before flinging it open to be greeted by an old bedraggled cat. It stared at her in bemusement, before turning and wandering back along the landings and down the stairs. She peered out of the door and squinted as her failing eyes attempted to see along the dark corridors. But there was nothing. She closed the door and shivered as she retreated back to the refuge of her bed.

"Damn cat," she muttered.

The wind continued to whistle through the cracks and crevices of the draughty interior, but to the unsuspecting world outside Juniper House remained silently hidden in the shadows of Gallows Lane.

LATER

THE AIR GREW COLD as the wind gained strength, and night cast its spell over the hamlet of Judge Fields. Juniper House, with its tall gables, was hardly visible behind the overgrown and chaotic garden. It was still and silent but for the wind rattling at the loose window panes, and as it lay empty behind the tall weeds and grasses, so it was ignored by the residents of the few scattered houses in the village. But something sinister had remained long after the last occupant of Juniper had gone. Some form of communication had continued behind its walls, and a presence born out of pain, anguish and cruelty could not be extinguished by mortal will alone.

The house creaked and groaned as it battled the elements. Winter was taking its toll as the wind fought its way through every slit and chink, and every nook and cranny that could be found within the old stone walls, until it unmercifully invaded the empty interior. And as it howled through each nick and gap in the roof and rafters, the sound echoed in the hollowness of the vast spaces inside. The distant screeching of a door could be heard inside as it opened and closed, and soft footsteps were barely audible as they slowly made their way down the long dusty hallway and across the sitting room floor. An unexpected streak of lightning flashed through the gaps in the shutters and momentarily lit up the room to expose and warn any intruder of the oncoming storm, a threat that was soon to be realised as a loud crack of thunder ripped through the fabric of the building. But above the noise of the gale, a melancholy tune interrupted the atmosphere as the sound of a piano playing beautifully and melodically echoed hauntingly throughout the empty spaces. The straining of a rocking chair as it creaked on its hinges, could be heard moving in harmony, back and forth, to the soulful notes which filled the air and continued all through the night.

But during the storms of the night, and the calm of the day, to the unsuspecting world outside Juniper House still remained silently hidden in the shadows of Gallows Lane.

1

NOW

Anton and Lucy braved the cold weather as they packed some items into their camper van and decided to set off to a small and very remote village in Cumbria. It was, historically, part of the West Riding of Yorkshire, and could be found nestled in a narrow valley on the western slopes of the Pennines within the Yorkshire Dales National Park. It was one of their favourite places to visit, and there was a good Caravan and Camping site where they could pull in for the night.

There were several routes to choose from in order to get to the village, but there was just one which they had never tried before. It was a narrow, winding road which looked down on a remote valley; and whilst the road was picturesque, so they'd heard, it was not for the faint hearted. Always up for a challenge Anton was keen to try it out, and he'd had his map sprawled out on the floor earlier that morning, familiarising himself with the directions; while Lucy busied herself sorting out a few pots and pans.

"We go through a hamlet called Judge Fields, I know where it is. It's not far from that place we sometimes eat at, which is just on the borders; you turn off a lane just before it. Looks like there's a pub with food, and there's a small campsite and pull-in park too," he'd called to Lucy enthusiastically.

"Right, that's it, we know where we're going – easy-peasy this one!" He'd folded up his map and jumped up off the floor invigorated at the thought of setting off later, and Lucy was just as enthused.

They weren't fazed by the weather, they'd only had their camper van for the first season that year and they'd made the most of it; come hail or shine they were off every week-end. The season would soon be coming to a close and they wanted to make sure they did as many trips as they could before it all ended.

"Everything's packed," Lucy called, wondering where Anton had got to when he didn't respond. She walked through their tiny one-bedroomed-flat and peered out of the window to see Anton checking out their vehicle. She went outside to join him. He was her first real love, and she knew there couldn't ever be another. He was tall and lean, whereas Lucy was petite only measuring five foot two in her bare feet; she had to stand on her toes to put her arms around his neck and even that was a struggle. They had known each other for a year before they'd decided to set up home together. Both of them were mature enough to make sensible decisions, and living together was one of their wiser ones. They had met for the first time when she was twenty six and he was thirty two, at a dance club for country dancing. He had turned up perfectly dressed for the occasion, wearing a red check shirt, blue jeans, western style boots and a large Stetson. He had been the centre of attention, and the star of the show, when it came to showing off the dance routines. And he had chosen her to be his partner. They became dance buddies immediately; but it soon turned into something much more special. They got on like a house on fire, and had so much in common that it was inevitable they would fall in love.

"Is everything alright?" she asked hesitantly, as she watched him inspect the van.

"Err yes I think so." He was walking around it kicking the tyres. He was dressed in his normal attire of blue jeans, thick check outdoor shirt, and boots which looked like hikers. Other than wearing overalls for doing jobs and messing around, he never wore anything else. In fact he often bragged about his need for only three drawers and no wardrobes; one drawer for his socks and underwear, another for his shirts and tee shirts, and one for his jeans. He rarely wore a jacket, or coat of any kind, as he preferred his old woolly cardigan which always looked as if he'd slept in it – it had belonged to his granddad. His short, tousled fair hair complimented his boyish looks and seemed to magnify his soft blue eyes.

They'd had no problems with the van ever since they'd bought it back in the spring, and Lucy was hoping it would continue. It was quite an old vehicle, but Anton was pretty handy at sorting things out, after all he was an engineer so he had a fairly good understanding of anything technical, or mechanical, and he was a very practical person too.

After what looked to be a good inspection, he decided it was in perfect order and so he was itching to get going. Lucy packed a few final things in the drawers and cupboards of the vehicle, and locked up the flat. They were away well before lunchtime.

Anton soon spotted the turn-off which would take them through the hamlet of Judge Fields, so he turned into it. He drove up the narrow lane, passing a few ancient houses on the way, and within seconds they were passing The Old Inn.

"Looks a bit grotty," exclaimed Lucy with disappointment in her voice; although they were not planning on trying it out anyway, so as far as Anton was concerned it didn't really matter one way or another.

They soon came to a mediaeval church with a small graveyard to the front and side, in which there looked to be some very ancient headstones, so they slowed down to take a closer look.

"Have you seen the street-name on the wall?" Lucy said excitedly. "We're parked in Gallows Lane." She shuddered once its implications sank in, whilst Anton found it intriguing.

"That's an unusual name," he answered. "Do you think they might have hanged people around here in the past? Funny the hamlet's called 'Judge Fields' as well."

"I don't want to think about it!" she responded, cringing at the same time. She wasn't too enamoured with the hamlet, it was very remote, dead as could be, and there was a strange atmosphere in the air.

"This is the way to pick up the top road over to where we're going, so I can't imagine where they could erect gallows along here, if that's what they used to do."

"Maybe they used to string them up on the trees," she offered, half jesting. She pointed towards a high stone wall. "Look at all those trees on the left, maybe *they're* covering up something."

Anton set off again and drove slowly up to where the trees were. He stopped the engine and got out, whilst Lucy stayed inside the cab. He walked a few metres and then stopped. He called back for Lucy to join him. "Hey Luce, come here and take a look at this." He then seemed to disappear through the trees.

She stepped out and walked over to join him, and soon discovered that he was walking around someone's garden. She looked up at a very large and very ancient house with tall gables, which could hardly be seen behind the overgrown weeds and grasses. It was almost invisible from the roadside, as the overgrowth had almost reached to the bottom of the first floor windows. Although it stood in a substantial plot, the property looked to be in very poor condition. To its side was a wooden porch with no outer door, and the wood was rotting badly and almost looked as if it could drop to bits at any time. Anton had disappeared round the back somewhere, but Lucy decided to peer through the small window in the porch door. She had to rub hard to create a small area in the dirt-ridden glass in order to see through it. She was careful where she stood on the rotting platform of the porch, as she didn't want to lose an ankle through the gaps in the wood. She clung onto the door and leaned across at an angle, whilst keeping an eye on her feet. She put her eyes close up to the gap in the pane of glass and peered inside. She squinted as she tried to focus, the glass misting up with her warm breath. She could just make out a long hallway which was empty and bare of any carpets or mats. It looked to open out into a larger hallway at the very end, and she thought she could almost see the bottom step of a very wide staircase. She rubbed the glass again in an attempt to see more clearly, as everything seemed to blur as she struggled to see into the distance. She could hear Anton coming back, the sound of his shoes crunching as he walked over the long weeds and grasses and at that very moment she saw a movement down the hallway. She couldn't just make it out, so she squinted even more before realising that it was an old woman dressed in ragged clothes. She jumped back, almost losing a shoe in a crack in the rotting platform, and in her attempt to avoid it she lost her balance and fell backwards from the porch and into the overgrowth, just as Anton was approaching her.

He ran over and helped her to her feet. "Are you alright?" he asked in a worried voice.

Lucy brushed herself down and said, "Come on, let's get out of here. Someone is living here – I've just seen an old woman inside."

She rushed him outside and back to their vehicle. They both climbed inside and Anton started the engine; but he hesitated and sat there for a while.

"You must be mistaken Luce there's no-one in there, I've looked through the windows. It's empty but for a few sticks of furniture here and there. It's fascinating round the back though. I've just been exploring some old outbuildings, some of which looked to have been stables. You want to see the old bicycle – it's ancient. And there's an old washhouse, the likes of which I've never seen in my life. This place seems to have stood still in time. And what's more, there's an old estate agent's board lying in the undergrowth. It must've been there for years. I tried to pick it up, but it seems to have rotted in with all the weeds and everything. It has obviously been up for sale at one time or another and never sold." He was very excited.

"Well, I could've sworn I saw someone," she said, looking confused.

"No way, love. This place has been abandoned. It doesn't look as if anyone's been near it in years."

He began to turn the car round and head back the way they'd just come.

"What are you doing?" her voice raising an octave.

"I'm going into that old pub to ask some questions. We might as well have a drink whilst we're there. Maybe we could grab a sandwich or something."

"But it looked grotty – like I said!" She had never seen him this excited before, she didn't know what had come over him. And what was the point of asking questions? It was just a big old empty house, clearly unloved, and in her opinion – unfriendly too. And whether she saw anyone in there or not, hardly mattered. She would much rather they carry on their journey, which was, after all, the general idea.

But Anton was determined and he carried on and drove round to the back of the pub to some make-shift car parking area. He jumped out and beckoned her to follow. He marched over to the entrance and Lucy followed behind him, her small steps struggling to keep up with his long stride.

The inn was indeed very ancient, with flagged floors and lots of dark wood panelling and exposed stonework. The ceilings were also heavily beamed. As for the horseshoe bar, neither of them had seen one like it before, it seemed to have frozen in time. Pewter tankards of varying sizes were hanging from hooks around the top of the bar, and old fashioned beer pumps were still in use. But logs were blazing in a stone fireplace in the corner of a room which looked like a snug, and they were both immediately drawn towards it.

A middle-aged man appeared behind the bar and asked if they wished to order. He was unshaven and his grey hair was long and greasy. Across the other side they could see an old man standing at the corner of the bar, nursing a schooner of beer and eyeing them cautiously. Otherwise the place was empty.

Anton was keen to ask questions, but decided they'd better order something first.

"Are you serving food?"

The man didn't answer but simply pulled a menu from under the counter and passed it to Anton. He eyed them both suspiciously.

"Ah, thanks." He ushered Lucy to a seat near the fire and they both browsed the menu.

"It's not exactly welcoming here, is it?" he whispered to her.

Lucy just grunted in response – she was not impressed.

"Shall we order a sandwich?"

Lucy leaned over to him, pinched his arm, and hissed in his ear: "I don't want to eat here, it's grotty!"

"A sandwich should be okay. I'll order ham sandwiches and tea for both of us." And giving her no time to raise further objections, he got up and wandered over to the bar and placed the order.

Lucy couldn't understand what had come over him. Why on earth were they sitting in some grotty little pub, which was as dead as a doorstop, ordering food, when they should be on their way to their lovely little village which they both adored? It was so out of character for Anton. After a sharp intake of breath, she exhaled abruptly as she sighed in exasperation.

He came back with a huge smile on his face.

"I'll bet that old codger over there can tell us a lot about the house." He motioned over to the old man who was still standing at the far corner of the bar.

"What house?" Lucy asked, looking bewildered.

"The one we saw in Gallows Lane, silly!"

He pinched her cute nose gently, but she wasn't amused. He had got a bee in his bonnet about that house and she was already beginning to hate it. And she knew there was someone in it, she had seen her. What was the matter with him? What was it about that house which could make Anton forget all about their plans for the day? He was behaving like a complete stranger and she wasn't a happy bunny.

"If we act like normal customers and eat here, I'll feel more inclined to ask about the house. I wouldn't like to have just wandered in, not buy anything, and just start quizzing about it. And afterwards, we can have a nosey around that graveyard – it looks really ancient."

Lucy was speechless. He was getting excited again, almost delirious, and she couldn't fathom why. And she feared they were heading for an argument. They didn't argue, they had little tiffs now and then, but nothing serious, and he always gave in to her anyway. They shared everything together, so much so that all their friends couldn't understand why they chose to do everything on their own, without the benefit of any of them joining in. She was suddenly feeling very neglected.

It didn't take long for Anton to see how unhappy Lucy was looking. He tousled her short cropped chestnut hair and looked down at her elfin-shaped face which housed two very large hazel eyes. He tipped her chin towards him. "I'm sorry love, but that house has been up for sale and it's obvious that it never sold. It looks as if it wants some work doing on it, and if I can find out who owns it, I think we might be able to bag a bargain."

"But I didn't know we were looking for a house," she responded sulkily.

"We weren't, but having come across that one, it's started me thinking. Whoever owns it must be glad to get rid of it, surely. It must be a liability to them and it's obvious that no-one's looking after it."

"But what about the old woman I saw?" her voice threatening to reach higher notes than normal.

"There's no old woman Luce, you must be mistaken."

"But I saw her, I know I did!" She was adamant.

Anton wrapped his strong arm around her shoulders and gave her a squeeze. "Just think about it Luce, if we bought it I could do it up whilst we live in the van in the grounds."

He very quickly became aware of the look on her face, and astutely changed tactics.

"On second thoughts, we could probably make one or two rooms in the house habitable for the winter and just use the van in the summer." The likes of which didn't exactly appeal to her either.

"What about the flat?" she asked in dismay. She was confused. Anton was moving too fast for her and she couldn't get her head round what he was planning. And whatever it was she didn't like the sound of it too much.

"The lease comes to an end soon, so we could continue to rent a month at a time until we complete the transaction on the house."

"But you don't know how much it would cost – how do we know we could afford it?" she gasped, her eyes opening as big as golf balls.

"I know we can, just call it gut-feeling. We have enough saved to cover a deposit and more. And I have an estimate in my head as to what I think I should offer for it."

"But we haven't even seen inside!" She was quickly becoming fearful that she was about to lose this argument, and suspected that Anton had temporarily lost his marbles.

"I've seen enough Luce. I had a good look around and peered through some of the windows. The roof is sound enough and those outbuildings offer a lot of potential. They would make good holiday lets, or alternative accommodation. We could even open a B&B and extend the accommodation by converting the outbuildings. I can do a lot of the work myself at week-ends and evenings, and there's enough land to grow our own produce on and to have a few chickens – we would almost be entirely self-sufficient. That roof's ideal for solar panels and I've got loads more ideas. We could get a loan on the basis of the value of the house once it is refurbished and modernised, plus the potential for business. We would probably qualify for a grant too because of the tourist attraction value."

Lucy was speechless. She could see that he was losing himself in a world of fantasy. He was fast-forwarding so furiously that he couldn't keep up with himself, or his thoughts. Anton was normally always the strong arm she could lean on, she had total faith and confidence in anything he did for the two of them, and she was normally happy for him to make most of the decisions. He was her rock, but this time she wasn't convinced. And she wasn't sure she fancied a B&B, or holiday lets in this rather unfriendly hamlet. And although they had talked about it before, she'd never had to think of it seriously – until now. And she wasn't sure that she was too keen on the idea. Talking about it and actually doing it, were two very different things in her opinion. Although she had to admit that her little job at the hotel, near to where they lived at Kirkby-Lonsdale, didn't pay much; but it did give her the benefit of part-time flexible hours. And as Anton believed that he should be the provider, it suited her fine. She was home in time to cook dinner and to have their little flat all nice and cosy for when he came home from work, and she was never under any pressure – so life was nice and easy. She wasn't sure she wanted to spoil it. And although she wasn't afraid of hard work, her relationship with Anton was perfect the way it was. They had all that they wanted as far as she was concerned – and they were happy.

The conversation didn't go any further, because the man returned with their sandwiches. He put them down on the table and returned to the bar.

"Do you think there's only him here?" asked Lucy, nodding towards him disapprovingly.

"It's hard to say! We're in at the early doors, so maybe none of the staff have arrived yet."

"Nor have the customers," she grunted.

He gave her a quick cuddle of reassurance. "Don't worry Luce I have it all under control."

She grunted again as she picked up her sandwich and scrutinised it. Anton's blue eyes twinkled wickedly as he picked up his sandwich, parted it slightly, and operated it with both hands to behave like a pair of teeth, which caused Lucy to burst into a fit of laughter. Needless to say, her mirth caught the attention of the barman and his one other customer, who both stood by silently and stared. However, Anton loved to see her pretty face light up when she smiled, or laughed, and he adored her for it. He knew his ideas would excite her once she came round to his way of thinking, and she would – he was determined.

He stood up, and without saying a word walked over to the bar and asked for half a pint of lager. He stretched his lean body across the counter-top casually, and addressed the barman at the same time as the old man.

"Can you tell me anything about the empty house up in Gallows Lane?"

The barman stopped drawing the lager for a second, and the old man seemed to show a flicker of concern in his eyes.

"Why do you want to know?" the barman asked gruffly.

"I'm interested in buying it."

The barman remained silent as he filled the glass with lager. He slid it across the counter to him and gave him a cold stare. Anton was not one to give up easy, so he paid the man, sipped at his drink and spoke again.

"I can see it was up for sale once, but it's empty, so presumably it was never sold?"

"Go look somewhere else!" he snapped, turning away abruptly and trying to look busy behind the bar.

Anton picked up his glass and walked round to where the old man was standing. He noticed he was nursing an inch of beer in the bottom of his.

"I'll have the same again for this chap," he called across the bar. But he was being given the silent treatment. He then turned to the old man. "Sorry mate, I don't know your name?"

But if he was expecting to find out, the old man wasn't forthcoming; but he accepted the drink willingly.

"I take it you live around here?" Anton asked, as he made a further attempt to converse.

"What's it to you?" The old man lifted the glass to his lips, gulped down a large amount of the beer, and eyed Anton shiftily.

Anton was flummoxed for a second. He wasn't really expecting an answer. Now he'd got him talking, he intended to take full advantage. "So you'll know who owns the old house?"

"Maybe!" he replied flatly.

"So, how do I get in touch with them?"

"You'd be wise to leave it alone."

Anton's curiosity was now aroused and he was feeling like a dog with a bone, he didn't intend to give it up.

"Is that because it's in such poor condition?"

The old man studied Anton and sipped at his drink.

"It's a wicked house. No good will come of it. Best left alone." He spoke more vehemently this time.

"Well I intend to make it a less wicked house. What do you think about that?"

The old man didn't answer.

"Well I don't believe in wicked houses, and if you can't, or won't tell me whose house it is, I'll find out elsewhere." Anton drank back the lager and put his empty glass on the bar top. But as he turned to walk away the old man spoke again, and stopped Anton in his tracks.

"I've got the keys."

Anton spun round and stared at him in astonishment. He couldn't believe his luck. Had he heard him right, or was he hearing things?

"You've got the keys?" he asked in amazement, his face a picture of delight.

The old man dug his hand into his jacket pocket and pulled out a bunch of keys on a large key ring. He dangled them under Anton's nose. "Here, take them. Take a look at it. You won't like what you see."

Lucy had been taking it all in, and at that point she stood up and walked across to the bar.

"Hey, what about the old woman who's in there, I've seen her?"

The old man clung onto the keys as if to retract them, just as Anton was about to grasp them from his hand.

"What old woman?" His voice trembled and his face turned ashen.

"The one I saw down the hallway when I looked through the glass in the door."

Anton didn't normally get mad at Lucy, but he was rather wishing she'd kept her lovely mouth firmly shut. "Ignore her, she's very imaginative," he said, reaching for the keys again.

"No I'm not imaginative – I saw her! She was very old and dressed in rags, and she peered at me from the bottom of the hallway." Lucy had assumed a rebellious stance and Anton didn't like it.

He looked across at her and gave her an instructive look, which she ignored. She was now on her high-horse and couldn't be stopped.

"Does she live there alone?" She intended to get an answer.

By now the barman was standing to attention and watching all that was going on. He too looked quite ashen and he shifted his feet uncomfortably.

The old man almost threw the bunch of keys into Anton's willing hand. He knew they weren't going to give up easily, and he wanted to get them away and out of the place altogether.

Anton held the keys with a feeling of satisfaction. He had not only achieved what he had come for, but far more than he'd expected, and he couldn't wait to get out of there and back to the house to explore.

But Lucy had no intentions of going into that house if someone was living in it – or maybe squatting in it. She hadn't thought of her being a squatter before now. However, she thought she would have one more try.

"So, are you going to tell me who that old woman is?"

"There is no old woman," he called back gruffly. "At least not anymore," he muttered in a hushed voice, much too quiet for Lucy or Anton to hear. If they had heard the old man's comments, Lucy may well have put her foot down and refused to go back there.

2

BEFORE

THE WOMAN STOOD INSIDE THE PORCH waiting rather impatiently for someone to answer the door, but no-one came. "Shut up Prissy!" she hissed at the howling cat. She began to shiver as the cold gripped, it was late November and she had been on the road all day. She was tired and irritable, and the cat had done what it had to do in its basket and wasn't happy – nor was the taxi driver she recalled. So all in all, there were some unhappy faces that day. She squinted through the dirty glass pane in the top half of the door and saw the old woman at the bottom of the hallway peering back curiously.

"Open up Mother, it's me – Beryl."

"What do *you* want?" asked a faint voice from the distance.

"I want to come in. Now stop dithering and open the door."

The old woman hesitated, and then shuffled towards the door. She put her face up to the glass and stared. "Oh it *is* you," she muttered.

Beryl could hear the sliding of three bolts, and a key turning in the lock. The door creaked open, but only to the width the safety chain allowed.

"What do you want?" she hissed. Then her eyes looked down on three large suitcases, before her poor hearing was disturbed by the sound of a screeching cat. She turned her gaze to the ginger and white animal in the basket, and slammed the door shut again. On went the bolts once more and she turned to shuffle back down the hallway.

Beryl put the basket down and forced open the letterbox which had clearly been taped down. She lifted the flap and shouted down the hallway: "Mother, come back, I've travelled a long way to see you. I've come to stay."

The old woman stopped dead in her tracks.

"Who says?" she said, as she turned her head back towards the door, her voice strengthening as she spoke.

Beryl realised she would have to change her tactics if she didn't want to remain glued to the porch platform. "I've come to stay with you for a few days. I'll make you a nice cup of tea."

The old woman hesitated before choosing to go back and open the door. She opened it cautiously, a little at a time.

"Is Billy with you?" she asked hopefully.

"Beryl pushed the door open and forced her way in, almost knocking the old woman over in the process. She put the cat basket on the hall floor and dragged her suitcases in one at a time.

"Billy isn't coming – he's never coming back you silly old fool."

The old woman looked bewildered and her face saddened. She stood and watched her daughter pull the suitcases on their castors, along the hallway and over to the bottom of the stairs. She started to drag them up the stairs one by one, as if she had every right to and as if the old woman didn't exist. The cat by now had gone quiet, and the old woman glared at it.

"I'm allergic to cats," she whimpered. But no-one was listening. She hobbled back to the scullery and sat down in the old rocking chair which was placed in front of an old black Yorkshire range. But there was no fire burning in the grate, it was just black and cold. She pulled a blanket around her frail body in order to keep warm and began to rock slowly, drifting back into her solitary world of sadness and heartache.

"I'm allergic to cats," she mumbled to herself. "Are we having a cup of tea?" Her voice trailed off to a quiet murmur as she rocked the chair gently. A faint smile spread across her features, as she repeated over and over again: "Billy's coming home soon."

And then a tear trickled slowly down her cheek.

3

NOW

STANDING OUTSIDE THE PUB Anton dangled the keys temptingly at Lucy, his face beaming. But she wasn't sharing his enthusiasm, on the contrary – she wasn't too keen on entering a house whose ownership they knew nothing about.

"We can walk back up the lane, it's not far," he beckoned, as he set off walking.

Lucy followed behind him, dragging her feet to show her obvious dissatisfaction. Anton turned round and smiled amusingly at her. Her head was bowed to the ground as she walked, and he caught her arm as she reached his side. Putting his big strong arm around her shoulders, he hugged her to him as they walked together up the solitary lane which took them past the ancient church and to the big old house on the opposite side of the road. As they arrived at the entrance Anton stopped. Once upon a time there would have been a gate in place, supported by the two stone posts, but it had obviously long since disappeared. He pushed some of the overhanging branches away from the post on the left side of the entrance, and saw a name engraved in the stonework. It read 'Juniper'. He walked across to the other side, his arm still wrapped protectively around Lucy's shoulders as he led her along, and as he expected the name on the other post was 'House'.

"Juniper House, Gallows Lane, Judge Fields," he said smugly. "It's a good name, a good address, and I have a good feeling about it. I think we're destined to have this house Luce, I can feel it beckoning. Come on, let's get inside. I can't wait, it's so exciting. Just think this could be the beginning of the rest of our lives together."

Lucy shrugged, but had nothing to say. Anton unfolded his arm from around her small shoulders and walked over to the door in the porch. He fiddled with the keys until he found the right one, and although it turned in the lock it wouldn't open. He tried the remaining keys but without success. "I think this door must be bolted. It makes sense when you think about it, because the door's so rotten it would easily break down if someone wanted to rob this place." But his nonchalant comment provoked Lucy out of her sulk.

"Why would someone want to rob *this* place – rob it of what?" Lucy sneered.

"Oh, you'd be surprised love. There's plenty to attract someone to an empty house, I can assure you. C'mon, let's try round the back." He marched off quickly and before Lucy had time to catch up, he was already in at the back door. "I'm in!" he called to her and then disappeared. Lucy didn't much care to be left out there alone, so she rushed to get in behind him.

The house was musty and dark, but their eyes soon accustomed themselves to the dimness.

"You should've brought the torch from the van," Lucy whispered uncomfortably.

"You don't need to whisper love, there's no-one here – except of course, the bogey-man!" He made a scary move towards her, but instead of smiling she gave him a dirty look. She felt as if they were trespassing. It may be empty to him, but as far as Lucy was concerned it felt as if it belonged to someone else – and of course in reality it still did.

"I don't think we should be here. If the house doesn't belong to that old man, who does it belong to? We should have got permission from the owner and perhaps then someone would have guided us around." She was still whispering.

Anton's excitement couldn't be dampened. They were in a darkened passageway at the back of the house. It contained an old pot sink on a metal pedestal which was fixed firmly to the stone floor. It was like stepping back in time. He pushed open a door which led into what appeared to be an old scullery with another stone floor.

"Hey, Luce, come and look at this." He took a box of matches from his pocket and lit one.

"I'm right behind you," she whispered nervously, as her fingers gripped his shirt for support. She had no intentions of straying anywhere without him inside a house with no electrics and looking like the black hole of Calcutta.

He was staring at an old, black, Yorkshire range, in front of which stood an ancient looking and well-worn rocking chair. An old woollen blanket which was grey in colour was strewn on the floor. Above the range was a large clothes rack suspended from the ceiling, a few odds and ends still visibly clinging to it.

"This will be worth a fortune," he said eagerly.

"What will?" she asked sarcastically, her voice now at full volume.

"This Yorkshire range, you don't see many of these anymore." He winced as the match burnt his fingers before dying a death, and he quickly dropped it on the floor and lit another.

But Lucy wasn't impressed, and she didn't like being in the house either. She still felt like a trespasser and she also felt as if they were being watched. She looked around just in case, but of course they were alone – she knew that deep down inside. But her mind still wandered back to the old woman who she thought she had seen earlier.

Anton led her through to the next room. As he stood in what looked to be the main sitting room, he stared around in amazement. It was a big room with lots of daylight coming in from two large windows which had wooden shutters held back in place. The floor was bare of carpet and there were no window dressings either. But Anton's attention was focused on a grand piano which stood in the far corner of the room. It was covered in decades of dust, which had weaved itself together, over time, to form what looked like a fisherman's net draped across it. It must have been left alone and abandoned for a lifetime to end up in that condition. A piano stool with a well-worn upholstered seat was placed in front of it, and apart from one sheet propped up on the music rest, others were scattered around the floor. Everything was in the same condition as the piano.

There was an old bookcase full of books positioned against a wall, and the odd chair here and there, plus a big old-fashioned dining table, but not much else. He walked over and browsed through the books, they were mainly educational, many of which were books on art and sculpture, but they were badly damaged with mould and mildew and were hardly legible.

He picked up some of the deteriorating music sheets and placed them on the top of the piano stool carefully, as if he'd been appointed as custodian of someone's treasures. And they probably had been someone's treasures once.

They walked into a rather grand old hall with an ancient, wide, curved staircase with very old spindled balustrading. None of it bore any sign of carpets, just exposed wood. The dark, bare and deteriorating walls showed only dim signs of faded paintwork which was grey with age and soiled heavily from years of neglect. Cobwebs hung from every corner and were draped loosely from ceiling to wall. Someone must have once helped themselves to all of the carpets, as even old houses often have threadbare remains. But this house had nothing apart from dust and cobwebs which were plentiful.

Lucy felt as if she'd walked into someone else's past, it was grim and scary, and she wished Anton would get the hell out of there and retreat to the comfort of their van and get on with their planned journey for the day.

"C'mon Luce, I can't wait to see what it's like upstairs." He beckoned her to follow, as he bounded up the stairs two steps at a time until he reached a long arched window at the half-return. He stopped to inspect.

"Look Luce, this window is all intact – it's in pretty good nick. That's good, cos it would be a dreadful shame to have to replace all this beautiful leaded glass with something more contrived."

Although Lucy couldn't manage to do the steps two at a time like Anton, her fear of the house overwhelmed her lack of interest, so instead of lagging behind she ran up them as quick as she could. But by the time she had caught up to him, he was off again bounding up the remaining steps until he reached an enormous landing which branched off in at least two directions. He strutted around trying all the doors and peering out of the grimy windows to survey the grounds, the views, and the surrounding countryside. By the time Lucy caught up with him again, she found him standing in front of a door eyeing it suspiciously.

"What's so fascinating about that door?" she asked breathlessly.

"Take a look at it, what do you see?"

"I see a door, what am I expected to see? Surely you don't think I can see through it – do you?"

"Seriously Luce, doesn't something strike you as odd?"

She stared at it again, willing it to talk to her because she hadn't a clue what she was supposed to be looking for, and quite frankly she didn't give a toss.

"It's been sealed up, that's what! Look, there's no handle and no lock; it's all been filled in."

Lucy felt a cold shiver run down her spine.

"I don't like it Anton, let's get out of here. This place is giving me the creeps."

"That's because you're a woman. It's perfectly natural for you to feel like that," he replied nonchalantly. "You women are all the same."

Lucy's mouth dropped open. She wasn't too much pleased about that chauvinistic remark. It was completely out of character for Anton – or was it? Perhaps she had never really noticed before that he was a little chauvinistic. She liked to think he had a strong, macho personality which made her feel protected and safe – now she was having doubts. Her expression was showing signs of a pout and Anton was quick to notice.

"Have I said something wrong?" he quizzed.

But she just shrugged her shoulders. This house was coming between them already, she thought, but she couldn't quite put her finger on it. It was clouding her vision and she was seeing something different under his skin. Oh God, how she wished they would get out of there. She could see their planned day going to the dogs. Time was moving on and they were getting nowhere.

Anton seemed to get the message.

"Come on Lucy, buck up. This is a chance in a lifetime, you'll see. Follow me and we'll inspect all the other rooms and then we'll leave. We'll hand the keys back to the old chap and then move on."

Lucy felt relieved and happy to hear him say that, because she was beginning to believe that the house was taking control of him and she was starting to feel increasingly worried. She knew she was possibly being neurotic by feeling that she was playing second fiddle to a house, but that's how it made her feel. The sooner they got out of there the better. She just hoped he would have got it out of his system by the time they handed the keys back. She sure didn't want to think about living in it – a thought which made her visibly shudder.

Having locked the house up and made it as secure as they could, they wandered back to the pub hand in hand. They didn't stop to look at the graveyard, as the rain was coming on and the skies had grown quite dark. It was getting late and they had already missed the chance of reaching their destination before daylight disappeared altogether. Anton moved faster as the rain became quite heavy, and Lucy had to run to stay beside him as his hand tugged at hers. They almost ran into the pub together, and although the barman was still there the old man had disappeared.

"Where is he?" Anton asked, trying to shake the rain off his tousled head.

"He's gone!" he grunted.

"I can see that," he responded downheartedly. "When will he be back?"

"After seven, when we open again."

"Does that mean you're closed?"

"That is correct! No-one comes in at this time of year."

"I can see that," he moaned again. "So what about these keys then?"

"You'll have to try again after seven."

"I know you've just told me that. So can I leave them with you?" Anton asked impatiently.

"Nope!" And with that the barman proceeded to lock up as he manoeuvred Anton and Lucy towards the door. Anton didn't offer any objection, after all he hardly wanted them both to be locked in that place for the rest of the day. And Lucy's face was a picture of annoyance, so he knew he was going to be in big trouble.

They hurried back to the camper van and jumped inside. The rain had come down quite hard and the skies were threatening a storm.

Anton drove back round the way they'd come in at the outset, and headed towards the pull-in which he'd seen earlier. He jumped out and went in search of a friendly face, but couldn't find anyone. Everything was closed up – everything except the toilet and shower block. He got back in the van and drove over to a space which he decided was suitable to park up in. He avoided looking at Lucy as he could see her face was competing with the stormy skies above. He knew it wouldn't be long before he had to face both storms – the latter of which he was not too keen on.

"And what are we doing here?" Lucy glared at him.

He was behaving sheepishly and he couldn't bring himself to look into her face. His mind was working overtime, as he searched for ways to make amends. It wasn't going to be easy. So better to just get on with it and face the music.

"We'll have to stay here for the night love. I'll have to give that old chap these keys back, but by the time the pub opens and he comes back in we'll be too late to go anywhere." *There, that wasn't too bad was it?* He thought to himself.

But her response came like thunder.

"It's that house isn't it? You want to stay so you can quiz him again. I know what your intention is – you only care about that stupid old house. I might as well not be here for all I seem to matter in this master plan of yours." *There – she'd said it, and she felt much better for getting it off her chest.*

Anton felt too guilty to argue because he knew she was right. He couldn't explain it, but the house was getting under his skin; he felt as if he belonged there – like coming home from a long voyage. He couldn't give it up, he just couldn't. He had to have it, no matter what it would take. He had no intention of backing down, because he had to do this for the two of them – it was destiny. He thought about it for a moment; could he really say in all honesty that he wouldn't bother about it anymore if Lucy said no? He shrugged that thought off, as he didn't want to face the truth.

"At least the toilet and shower block is open love."

"Don't you *love* me," she exploded. "I don't want to spend the rest of the day here and I certainly don't want to spend a night in this dead dump."

They both sat in silence for the next five minutes, each one waiting for the other to speak first. He knew Lucy would be in a real sulk for the rest of the week-end if he didn't do anything about it.

"We could check if they have rooms at the inn?" he tried to jest.

"I don't find that in the least bit funny," she fumed. "And I had to hide my sandwiches behind a cushion."

He hadn't known that! He thought she'd eaten them quickly come to think of it. And what had happened to *his* sandwiches? He'd got so wrapped up in viewing the house that he'd forgotten all about them.

"Did you hide mine too?" he asked, looking straight into her face.

Lucy took one look at him and burst into fits of laughter. He looked so forlorn when he said it that she couldn't stay mad at him any longer. They both cracked up together.

Anton wrapped his arms around her and gave her a big hug and a kiss.

"I'm sorry Luce. You're right of course, you always are. I've been a selfish sod all day, ever since I saw Juniper House. But I haven't meant to push you out, really I haven't. It's just that – well, I guess I just got so excited about it all. If you don't want me to mention it again, I won't – I promise."

She looked at his pleading face and melted. "Oh, okay, we'll stay the night and see what he has to say about the place when the pub opens."

She knew she had relented against her better judgement, but she could see the day wearing on and they simply weren't getting anywhere.

"Really – are you serious?" His face almost lit up the dark sky.

"Yes, but I'm going to rustle up something to eat first. I've packed a few tins of things and we've got eggs and bread. And I'm hungry!"

Anton grabbed her again and gave her a long loving kiss. "At least it will be intimate here we've got the whole place to ourselves. We can do anything we want."

Lucy looked at him suspiciously and curled her lip. But she preferred not to make any comment on his dubious remarks – her look said it all.

"Right let me sort out some food, I'm ravenous."

"Yeah me too, this house-hunting has made me work up an appetite."

Lucy frowned as she disappeared into the back to conjure up something to eat. She sighed to herself. She strongly suspected, as well as feared, that this house was going to be theirs no matter what; so she may as well start getting used to the idea. She knew Anton well, once he got a bee in his bonnet there would be no turning back.

4

BEFORE

As Beryl approached the landing she stopped to get her breath back. The final suitcase had been deposited on the floor while she sat on the top step for a rest. Although she was in her sixties, she had acquired the demeanour of someone much older. The first sight of her mother, after all the years that had passed, was a shock. She had changed, that was true, but they would now pass for sisters, not mother and daughter, as the difference in their age was no longer apparent. Where her own hair was a stern grey, her mother's was a gentle white which matched her personality as she remembered her. It wasn't that her mother looked younger than her years; it was the fact that she herself looked much older than someone in her sixties.

Beryl had never married. Born a spinster, she would die a spinster, of that there was no doubt. Well it's too late now, what's the use of worrying. Her mother, Magdalena, had become a recluse, so what good had marriage done for her? It had only caused her pain and sorrow, as far as Beryl was concerned. She'd had two children, but her life came to an end when her husband – Beryl's father – had left one day and taken her younger brother Billy with him. They were never seen again. He didn't even have the nerve to face up to what he was planning.

It had all happened when Magdalena had taken Beryl to London to be auditioned by a renowned master-of-ballet. He had been one of the greatest dancers the world had ever known and many world-famous ballerinas had been trained by him. He was one of the most sought after ballet teachers in the world. Beryl had only ever shown the one talent – she could dance. And it was her dream to become a world-class ballerina. But the short visit which had been planned turned into a week, due to them visiting an ailing aunt. Beryl's excitement at being told she had a special talent, was advanced for her years, and should start with the school as soon as possible, was beyond her wildest dreams.

But it all came to an abrupt end when they returned home. The house was grimly silent and Magdalena's husband, Sinclair, and her son Billy had gone and their clothes and personal belongings cleared out. Magdalena was devastated, and Beryl's dreams of becoming a dancer were gone forever.

Beryl blamed it all on Billy, whilst Magdalena blamed the loss of her son on Beryl; after all, if they'd never gone to London in the first place, none of it would have happened. Nothing was ever the same again and her dreams of being a ballerina were crushed.

From that day on Beryl and her mother grew apart. Magdalena adored Billy. He was the youngest of the two children and the apple of her eye. But he was also a musical genius; a gifted child who was being trained as a concert pianist. His playing was already concert material by the time he was two years old, and he would conduct his mother in time as she played. He was born a genius, and he was being studied carefully for a future career on the world stage. And although Beryl had been a talented dancer from a very young age, she didn't compare to the favoured member of the family, Billy. His amazing talents not only excelled in music, but he began to show the same artistic flair as his mother too, which all added to the admiration and pride she felt for him as she nurtured his abilities.

Beryl, however, had always dreamed of impressing her father, and whilst he had never shown great paternal instincts to any of his children, she knew she was more like her father than her mother, and therefore leaned more towards him rather than try to compete with Billy. She couldn't wait to impress her father when they returned with the good news from London. But it wasn't to be. Her father and brother were never seen again.

Magdalena never recovered from her son's loss. He was only six years old when he was taken by his father and no-one ever knew their whereabouts, or what had happened to them. They were written off by the authorities eventually and no-one knew if they were dead or alive.

As for Beryl she was only ten years old and *her* loss was two-fold. Not only had she lost the only chance she had to become a dancer, she had also lost the one person who she could relate to – her father.

From then on life was intolerable and empty for Beryl. She watched her mother's decline, as all interest in life was gone. She more or less had to fend for herself, as well as taking care of her mother for what it was worth. But she was unable to fix things as Magdalena was inconsolable. Seven years later Beryl left too, to seek her fortune in London. She simply packed a few things and walked out of the door and never came back. They were never in touch again.

Beryl had no conscience because she was her father's daughter. She felt no remorse and didn't have a problem putting her own interests before anyone else's feelings. She never stopped to think about what would happen to her mother, she didn't really care. Her own draw to London had a stronger place in her heart than any family interest. She had followed in her father's footsteps and abandoned her mother by walking out of the family home without as much as a word. And she didn't even bother to leave a note. She was convinced that her mother wouldn't even notice she'd gone anyway – and too heartless to even care.

Now she was back and she intended to claim what was rightfully hers. She had heard through the grapevine that the house had been burgled so many times over the years that there was hardly anything left inside it. Apparently rumours were rife that the old woman 'had lost it' and wouldn't have any idea if anyone slipped into the house. Now Beryl had returned she could see that the rumours were genuinely founded. The house didn't resemble the once grand house she had left behind all those years ago. It had clearly suffered from the elements and neglect over those many years. And it was now hard to imagine her mother being the competent musician and pianist that she'd once been, as well as having taught Art and Sculpture. She had been a very talented sculptress and had held many exhibitions in London, her sculptures being widely sought all over the world.

Magdalena had been very beautiful, articulate and well-educated. She was sophisticated and refined, which made it more the pity that Beryl hadn't followed in her footsteps; but she was too much like her wayward father. She silently recalled her tall, slim, debonair father with his trim black moustache and smooth short black hair. He could turn on the charm like the flick of a switch and women couldn't resist him. Behind the cultured façade he was a callous rogue, squandering mother's earnings on gambling and alcohol. He would disappear for days on end without any of them knowing where he was. Her mother tried to cover for him of course, knowing all along what he was, but she was a firm believer that if you make your bed you must lie in it. And so she continued to fund his extravagant lifestyle in the manner he enjoyed, for the purpose of shielding the children from the truth.

But Beryl always knew what he was up to – at least she'd always been sharp-witted enough for that. But Billy was much too young to know and he was too focused on his music anyway. He was just like mother with his ice-blue eyes and blonde hair, and he looked to be inheriting his mother's good looks as well. But Beryl was not as fortunate in that respect. Her hair was a boring mousey-colour – often the result of having a mother with blonde hair and a father whose hair was black. She'd also had the misfortune of coming somewhere in between when the looks were handed out. She'd always felt that she was a misfit neither one thing or the other – and she was insanely jealous of perfect Billy. But jealousy breeds resentment and Beryl's position was no exception – she even gloated on the fact that he was gone.

It had dawned on Beryl as the years passed, that her father had probably found another financially-secure woman of his choice, and had seen Billy as a meal-ticket for his own future. He'd probably thought that by stealing him away he would be guaranteed security in his later life, while he continued to live his rampant lifestyle with, no doubt, his new conquest. But although she herself had tried to locate him she had always come up against a dead end, until finally she gave up. And as she'd never been drawn to children, or to motherhood itself, she was unable to understand Magdalena's emotions and devastation and therefore had been unable to offer any support, or kindness, that might have helped her on the road to recovery. And quite frankly, she'd never really cared either.

She dragged herself up off the step and wheeled the suitcases one by one across the long, bare landing. She glanced up at one particular door on the way past and noticed it no longer had a handle and the door itself had been sealed up. She automatically headed for her old bedroom. It hadn't been altered at all, except the carpets and the furniture had all gone; but there was an old mattress on the floor which would be better than nothing .Walking back along the landing she noticed that the floorboards still creaked from one end to the other – nothing much had changed in that respect. She remembered how no-one could sneak past that particular area without everyone knowing. She felt no emotion at any of her childhood memories and no fondness. She had a plan in mind and she intended to carry it out, and there was no place in her heart for nostalgia.

Once her belongings were in the bedroom, she wandered back downstairs. She needed to sort out her cat and she knew mother wouldn't like that as she'd always been allergic to them. As she walked into the sitting room, she glanced over to the grand piano which was still there in the same position as it had always been. It wouldn't exactly be an easy item to steal, and its lack of use over the years was evident by the cloak of cobwebs strewn across it. Of course no-one could possibly take it without the necessary equipment to move such a weight, or at least being noticed in the attempt. So that's probably why it still remained; but she doubted if mother had ever played since Billy had gone. There had also been a beautiful and rare antique musical clock which had always sat on top of the piano, but that was no longer there. A valuable and unique piece, it was elaborately decorated in black and gold, with two dials above the clock face giving a choice of settings. A cord drawn from the side would allow it to play a choice of music. But mother had it set at her favourite piece, which was the one that Billy had first learnt to play; a masterpiece which for a six-year-old was unheard of. She had listened to it constantly after Billy had disappeared, no doubt imagining him sitting at the piano playing for her. The haunting melody had almost driven Beryl mad. The thieves must have been canny to get that out of the place without mother knowing. She recalled how her mother had shut herself away, spending her days and nights in the rocking chair in the scullery, gazing into the fire and waiting for Billy to return. She had always believed that her husband would return with Billy once he ran out of money, and she never locked the front door just in case.

But they never came back.

5

NOW

Anton and Lucy had eaten in the van, tidied up, explored the hamlet, and wandered around the caravan park whilst waiting for seven 'clock to come so they could return to the pub and give the keys back to the old man. There wasn't a great deal to do to while away their time, as there was very little in the hamlet of interest and due to the time of year it was pretty dead. The weather was miserable, it had been constantly drizzling for most of the afternoon, and Lucy was feeling peeved that they had missed out on their planned day because of what appeared to be an old and decrepit empty house. They had returned to the van to read, but Anton was edgy and couldn't settle.

"Could we still not set off to our village after we've given the keys back?" Lucy asked hopefully.

"I had thought about it, but we couldn't take the planned route as it will be too dark and it's a road we don't know. We could go back and pick up the road which we normally take. We'll arrive there late, but we should still be able to pull in. Everything will be closed no doubt."

"The pub will be open."

"Yes I suppose we can always spend an hour in there and then have an early night. We can set off early to walk in the morning."

But Lucy knew his enthusiasm had somewhat wilted and she knew it was all due to Juniper House. She knew him well and it was obvious that his mind was permanently on that property. He had continually checked his watch, but only because he couldn't wait to get back to the old man to ask him more questions. She sighed, knowing full well that they would end up staying the night in the hamlet so he could explore again the next day. But whilst the house was drawing him in, she felt it was pushing her out.

Her mind continually focused on the old woman she'd seen when peering through the glass. They had stared at each other, albeit for only a few seconds. She was old and her clothes very ragged and she looked pretty feeble; but her face had an aged beauty about it, and although her eyes seemed younger than her years they were full of sadness. Her hair was white and reminded Lucy of freshly fallen snow, and there was a gentle elegance about her despite the rags which were hanging from her frail body. It's quite amazing how much detail the mind takes in within such a short space of time, and how much the memory retains. But the vision had remained with her, and left her with a feeling about it that she couldn't explain. That was the reason she had been so adamant about her existence.

She would much prefer to get out of there and away from it all. The house was unfriendly and uninviting, and whilst it was seemingly empty Lucy had felt a presence when she was inside it as if someone still lived there. Maybe she was being foolish, it was probably just an atmosphere about the house that had got under her skin, but it was deep enough for her to feel scarred already. She had begun to dwell on her relationship with Anton, how it all seemed too perfect, how perfectly matched they were, and how perfectly well they got on. But nothing remains perfect forever, she knew that, and deep down she also knew that eventually it would have to change, just like relationships do; but she didn't want that change just yet. Changes take place gradually over time – perhaps many, many years, and then they change into something stronger, deeper, and lasting. It was too soon for those changes yet, far too soon.

"It's seven o'clock – dead on!" Anton jumped up, interrupting her thoughts with a vengeance.

"But if the pub only opens at seven o'clock, surely the old man won't be hanging around waiting outside the door?"

"I bet he will be," replied Anton with an abundance of delight. "Do you want to stay here and read your book? You don't need to worry about getting cold and wet out there, I can go on my own whilst you stay here nice and comfy."

"It's cold in here," she snapped. "And I don't intend to sit in it on my own. Anyway, if you go in there by yourself, you may never come out until they shut." She jumped up off her seat and grabbed her coat.

"Aw, alright then, I thought I'd just check," he said downheartedly. He actually sounded disappointed, which didn't do much for Lucy's feelings.

They both walked round to the pub which took about five minutes, although if Anton had gone alone it wouldn't have taken so long due to his long stride – as he repeatedly told her as she lagged behind. Lucy was grumping all the way there, after all he'd made it pretty clear he didn't want her with him. She'd never seen him like this before – if they were on their way to the local pub back home, she'd be convinced he'd got another woman!

Out of breath and feeling a bit bedraggled, Lucy trailed behind him for the last few metres. The pub was shut and that made her feel even more exasperated. Luckily there was a stone porch which they could stand in out of the rain – which they had to do for twenty minutes in the cold.

The door finally opened and the familiar face of the barman appeared.

"You're at the early doors aren't you?" he grumbled.

"I've come to return the keys." Anton jangled them before his eyes with a mischievous grin on his face.

The barman grunted and went back inside.

"He obviously doesn't like customers," Anton whispered to Lucy as he led her into the pub.

"That's probably because he's not used to having any. I don't see why he couldn't have taken the keys from you yesterday, so he could've given them to the old man instead of us hanging around," Lucy complained. But then she was niggled by a troubling afterthought. "What if the old man doesn't come in?" she blurted.

"I never thought of that," Anton said, his face beaming.

"But you can't seriously think of holding onto the keys – can you?" Lucy had stopped in her tracks and was now glaring at him. She was beginning to think the real Anton had been taken over by someone else. What on earth had got into him?

"Well we can't stay here forever. We have to go home sometime. If the barman won't take responsibility for the keys, and the old man doesn't come back to-night, there isn't much choice but to hang onto them – unless you've got any bright ideas!"

"Now listen to me, if that old man doesn't appear by eight o'clock, I insist you leave those keys on the bar regardless of what that barman says – and we just go. It's as simple as that!"

Lucy's chin was tilted upwards as she raised her voice to him. But he just looked down at her and frowned.

"Don't give me that puppy-dog look either," she ordered, before finally gasping in frustration at him. "Anton you're impossible!"

She shook her head in defeat as she followed behind him.

Once inside the pub Anton ordered two lagers at the bar, after ushering Lucy to a seat near the fire.

"What time does he come in, you said he came in at seven o'clock?" Anton asked the barman, knowing full well that he'd had no intentions of opening at seven.

"I don't have control over his time."

The barman didn't sound much pleased as he slid the two glasses of lager across the counter and took the money from Anton.

"Well tell me where he lives and I'll go and drop them off."

"Can't do that," he said.

"Why can't you?"

"Because I have no right to disclose a customer's address, after all, you wouldn't like me to give your address to any Tom, Dick or Harry now would you?"

"But I'm not any Tom, Dick or Harry. After all, he gave me the keys and he'll want them back. If I disappear with them, surely he'd be more annoyed at you for not telling me where he lives?"

But Anton was being ignored and he was feeling tetchy.

"How come he has the keys anyway? Does he own it?" Anton had never thought of that before. But his question still didn't prompt an answer. There was something fishy about the whole thing.

"I don't get involved in that old place, and if you take my advice you won't either. Leave it alone," he growled. "No good will come of it, mark my words."

Anton picked up the drinks and sat down beside Lucy, who was sitting taking it all in.

He remained quiet as he sipped at his drink and they both sat in silence. Lucy was the first to speak, but only in a whisper: "I don't know what's going on around here, but I think we should leave and go home. I don't like this place, I don't like this hamlet and I certainly don't like that house."

Anton never spoke, he was deep in thought. Lucy looked at him and decided to drink her lager and keep quiet. She wished they'd never chosen to try out the new route. If they had gone their normal way they would never have known about that house, and they wouldn't be stuck here like two prunes. It had been such a miserable week-end up to now, the first bad one they'd had since buying the van and Lucy was feeling downhearted.

"We'll just leave the keys and go when we've had our drink. He can't do a thing about it," Lucy whispered again in an attempt to break the silence. But it didn't do any good, as Anton seemed to be in a world of his own.

A few minutes later the old man appeared at the bar and Lucy breathed a sigh of relief.

"There he is – the old man's just come in," Lucy exclaimed, giving him a sharp nudge in the ribs to jolt him back to reality.

Anton perked up immediately and a big smile spread across his face.

"I'll just pop over and give him the keys," he said with gusto. He took his lager with him, his face still beaming.

Lucy rolled her eyes as she sighed deeply. *Thank God something's wakened him.* She pinned her ears back and listened carefully to their conversation, as she heard Anton offer to pay for the old man's beer.

Anton dropped the keys on the bar and sipped at his lager. He waited awhile before saying anything as he didn't want the old man to clam up again. He chose his moment carefully.

"I'm really interested in that old house. I want to buy it and do it up. I can do the work myself and I know I can bring it back to the home it must have once been. It needs a lot of loving care and attention, and I know I can give it that. It shouldn't be left in that state, it's going to deteriorate badly over each winter and then it will crumble. It must belong to someone and you know who it is, otherwise you wouldn't have the keys."

The old man picked up his glass and took a long drink before placing it back on the counter slowly. He seemed to be deep in thought after the young man's words and he was considering them carefully. He liked him, his freshness, his enthusiasm, his innocence. He'd been like that once.

Anton didn't pressure him, but waited patiently whilst keeping him company with his drinking. He couldn't help wondering who the old man was. He didn't even know his name. What connection did he have with the house? What did he know? And why did he have the keys? There were so many questions to be asked, but now wasn't the right time. He couldn't judge his age, his worn-out-face was partially hidden by his unshaven growth and long white hair which had long since thinned out on top. But he was old, Anton was convinced of that. His stature was bent and twisted with time and his fingers knobbly at the knuckles. His clothes were very dated, as if worn and never changed. He didn't look as if he was long for this world, and his expression was one of remorse, tiredness and weariness. His eyes were faded and almost void of colour, and there was a certain air of sadness about him. Maybe he was a fugitive who had found this reclusive hamlet in which to spend his remaining years – or months – without being found. Or maybe he'd just had a hard life. Anton's imagination grew rampant as he waited for some response.

"It belongs to the authorities," he finally said in a low, gruff voice.

His answer came out of the blue and Anton was taken aback as he almost choked on the drink he had just tried to swallow.

The old man pulled a crushed sheet of paper out of his pocket and slid it to him. "That's who you need to contact," he said bluntly. He slid the keys back to Anton too.

"Am I supposed to keep the keys?" Anton asked in surprise.

"You need to be keeping an eye on it if you intend to buy it. The authorities aren't interested in it they're only interested in the money. They'll be glad of anything you offer them. Money, always money, that's all anyone's interested in these days. They'll be glad to see it go, you mark my words."

Anton was speechless and didn't know what to say. He picked up the keys and thanked him, but just as he lifted his glass to go and re-join Lucy near the fire, the old man spoke again but bitterly this time.

"They took the house to pay for the fees."

Anton put his glass back down and faced the old man. He was simply staring into his beer looking forlorn and soulful.

"Fees, what fees?" he asked, determined to get to the bottom of it.

Once again he patiently waited to see if the old man would answer or remain silent.

"For the madhouse, what do you think?"

Anton was taken aback. He wanted to know more but was hesitant to push his luck, so he waited and ordered him another beer. The man didn't offer any objection but took it willingly as usual. Anton leaned on the bar casually and sipped at his drink, hoping the old man would unburden his soul. It was clear that he was becoming distressed as he'd been relating the snippets of information to him, so he didn't want to push him any further and upset him needlessly. He waited patiently, happy to keep the old man company whilst Lucy sat in front of the fire relaxing and enjoying the heat – but with all ears listening.

"That's all anybody's interested in these days, money, always money. People don't matter anymore, just money, that's all, just money," he continually repeated. He lifted his glass to his lips and finished the beer.

Anton continued to remain silent, as he had now cottoned on that the old man would open up more if *he* kept quiet. And he was right.

"She got her comeuppance though, that she did, but it was a long time coming. She was a good-for-nothing, an old witch, but it all rebounded on her in the end," he mumbled to himself before retreating into silence again.

Anton had no idea who, or what he was referring to.

The barman was continually drying the same glass with a tea-towel, as he looked on with a perturbed expression on his face. He was the first to break the silence.

"Go back where you came from and leave him alone. Forget about the place and leave it be! Take heed of what I'm saying, because no good will come of it." His voice was angry and his manner harsh. "You'll regret the day you ever saw it!"

As for the old man, he was rambling to himself having seemingly forgotten about Anton at his side.

Anton had more sense than to ask him anything else. He felt sorry for him and there was something about him that he couldn't fathom. Although he looked like a tramp, or a vagrant, something in his speech, his manner, and his tone, gave the impression that he may have once enjoyed a more cultured lifestyle. For a man with such a dishevelled appearance, and worn out face, he had meticulously manicured nails. His fingers, which showed obvious signs of arthritis, were long and narrow and his nails neatly trimmed. An earlier glimpse at his feet showed him to be wearing a pair of well-polished shoes, which were in total contrast to the rest of his attire. He was a contradiction of sorts, and had an air of mystery about him which intrigued Anton. Perhaps life hadn't been too kind to him over the years and he had finally succumbed to age. Maybe he was a war veteran - who knows! Or maybe he reminded him of his old granddad, who had died when Anton was still young but had left a strong impression on him. Maybe he was just being nostalgic – or maybe the old man was just a vagrant after all and his melancholy mood was clouding Anton's judgement of him. They were all maybe's, but he couldn't deny he was curious about him. He knew he wasn't going to get to know anything more, either about him, or the house, or its former occupants. And what he had heard up to now hadn't made much sense either, and it had all sounded a bit bizarre.

It was clear that the old man had clammed up and so Anton left it at that. He returned to where Lucy was sitting and sat down beside her.

"Did you hear all that?" he whispered.

"Sure," was her response, but she added nothing to it. She too seemed to be deep in thought.

"I'm not sure what I'm supposed to do with these keys, but it means we can go back and explore it more whenever we like." Anton's mood seemed somewhat subdued.

"Don't you think you've managed to be conned into keeping an eye on the place as key-holder, now you're stuck with them?" she hissed at an astonished Anton. "What if the police hear of an incident and call upon the key holder to open up for them? You'll have a long way to come to do just that, won't you?"

He couldn't understand her lack of interest. Here he was hoping to negotiate with the authorities to purchase a property for less than a song, knowing she would love it once he'd restored it. She could have the business she'd always craved for, which was to open a B&B and holiday lets. The extra land which he had surveyed while walking around the grounds, would be ideal for nightly pull-ins. The potential was huge and he knew he was capable of doing most of the work himself. He'd weighed it up carefully. Granted, they would have to give up their nights and week-ends for a while, but it was worth it. No pain without gain after all. And he knew they would gain a lot. Unperturbed by Lucy's attitude, he mapped out his plans to her.

"We'll have to wait until Monday before I can contact the authorities. Just think Luce, in a month or two we may well find ourselves living in Juniper House." He leaned over and gave her a squeeze. "You're going to love it, really you are. You can choose how you want it all to look and you'll love designing the interior decorations. You know that's what you're good at. Please tell me you're excited about it, please," he pleaded. "We can even have a dog or maybe two. You've always said you'd like dogs – and maybe cats, the grounds are perfect for cats too. Perhaps some chickens?" he said, trying to tempt her. "We'll never be able to have anything so long as we live in the flat. And we can park the van at the door – just think how easy that will be when unloading the shopping, then we can sell it when the house is ready."

Lucy, meanwhile, had been staring at him in astonishment, but his last remark prompted an outburst which he wasn't prepared for.

"Sell it?" Lucy gasped. She was dismayed. "Why should we sell it?"

"Because we won't have time for it once the house is finished and we'll need something more practical anyway. We'll be busy setting up the business to get it up and running for starters, that's going to be a full-time job. Eventually both of us can work together permanently, once you've got it established. Just think about it Luce, it'll be great."

He was brimming with enthusiasm at his grand ideas, but Lucy was feeling worried. She suddenly had a sinking feeling in the pit of her stomach. She had never thought about them selling the van, they both loved it. They had only just started going places with it and they had talked and planned the next year and the next. Why was everything changing? She was feeling very disturbed. And she sure as hell didn't want to live in that awful house!

6

BEFORE

OVER THE NEXT FEW WEEKS Beryl tried to get some heat into the old place by lighting the fires in each room. She managed to rustle up plenty of old wood from the garden and the old stores outside, and it didn't take long to warm the place up. The Yorkshire range was used for boiling water and cooking just as they'd done when she was young, and some cheeriness was brought back into the house. Her mother continued her daily vigil of waiting for Billy to come home, wondering where he had got to as she sat and waited in her old rocking chair. She pottered around too in a fashion, and Beryl kept her happy by making her regular cups of tea which perked her up no end. She was, of course, being lulled into a false sense of security with the notion that her daughter was back to care for her, which was as far from the truth as one could get.

Magdalena had reached a stage in her life whereby normality had become what she had become. A sense of hope and longing began each day, as she waited in vain for Billy. She no longer knew what the past meant, because to her time did not exist. It ceased from the day she discovered that her husband had disappeared and taken Billy with him. She became unaware of any changes that were taking place in her solitary existence, and Beryl's presence became part of that normality. Her mind was suffering the decline that solitude condemns it to, which made Beryl's cruel plans so much easier to execute.

They dined on tins of soup, bread, and potatoes from stock, as Beryl had chosen not to venture out and risk meeting any of the villagers until absolutely necessary. It was important that she remain invisible, after all, she hadn't existed to the residents of Judge Fields up to now and she intended it to stay that way. And so she shared her mother's reclusive and frugal lifestyle and remained firmly indoors for the winter months – and no-one was the wiser.

Each and every night as Beryl slept soundly in her make-shift bed from the mattress on the floor, she would be awakened suddenly by the sound of the creaking floorboards as her mother crept towards the bedroom door, with the cat in tow mewing constantly. She would hesitate outside, a lone and solitary figure, as if listening for signs of life before calling in her frail voice: "Are we having a cup of tea?"

This would continue until Beryl finally jumped out of bed in defeat and impatiently followed her mother downstairs to make a drink. She would join her mother in front of the range drawing what little heat there was to be had from the burning embers, and drink cups of tea while listening to her ramblings about Billy coming home soon. Beryl put up with her ageing and wandering mind for the time being, by compensating herself that it wouldn't be for much longer.

Over the months that followed, Beryl began to put her plans in motion. There was only one thing that she had inherited from her talented and beautiful mother and that was her handwriting. They were both left-handed – the only trait they shared, therefore Beryl was able to sign any papers or documents that belonged to her, including cheque books, because their signatures were identical. Gaining power of attorney was easy, so everything went according to her devious and cruel plans. All the while her mother was oblivious to what was happening, as she was enjoying the warmth, the food, the regular cups of tea, as well as having some company in the house. Beryl's return had also strengthened her conviction that Billy too was due to come home.

And so she continued to wait, her mood somewhat more cheerful as she looked forward to her six-year-old son walking through the door to play her favourite piece of music on the piano. The music sheet and the piano stool had both remained in place, undisturbed, since the day he'd been taken, and everything still looked the same to Magdalena. Her own advancing years had not registered in her mind either, as time had stood still and her age with it. She waited, comforted by her own joy and belief in the impossible. Beryl avoided saying anything that would shatter her happiness, as she led her to believe that things were just as she thought they were. The more she drifted into her own world, the easier it was for Beryl to finalise her plans.

Some weeks later the peace, which for a while had calmed the atmosphere of Juniper House, was shattered. A vehicle turned up at the house, and two men wearing white coats entered the front door. They marched down the long hallway, across the main hall, and through the sitting room, to the scullery where the old woman dozed as she rocked in her chair. Beryl nodded to them, and without giving the old lady any warning they ruthlessly yanked her by the arms and dragged her screaming in terror from the house.

Beryl bolted the door behind them, and her mother's final pleas as she screamed for Billy disappeared into the distance. Mother and daughter never saw each other again – at least not while the mother was alive.

Beryl soon adopted her new role as owner of Juniper House with glee. Now she was rid of the old bat, she could relax knowing she was secure for the rest of her days. She knew her mother had always had a plot reserved in the church graveyard across the way for her burial when her time came, but Beryl made sure the authorities were instructed to have her cremated, regardless of her mother's religious views. So Beryl was able to inherit the plot reserved by the church, for when her own time came; after all there wasn't anyone else to care for her remains once she'd gone. Her cruel cunning appeared to have worked to perfection.

Several years passed and she'd heard that her mother had died in her late nineties. She had rigorously held on to life at the asylum in York, regardless of its cruel regime, firm in her belief that Billy would be coming soon. And so, year after long year, she would sit and watch from the window of her room expectantly; watching and waiting and never faltering in her conviction that one day he would appear.

Beryl continued to live the same reclusive and frugal life which she had become accustomed to in that short period with her mother. But life had not been kind to her, as arthritis made her less and less mobile. And as infirmity began to descend upon her, things began to happen – strange things, sinister things, things which made her start to fear her own shadow.

One night she mounted the stairs as usual, carrying a candle to light the way. She had never had the electricity connected, as she managed with the range for most of her needs in respect of boiling water, cooking and heat, which no doubt had exacerbated the oncome of arthritis. Climbing the stairs was becoming more difficult, and she was relieved to reach her bed and practically fall into it after blowing out the candle.

She fell into a deep sleep but was abruptly wakened by the sound of creaking floorboards, as if someone was walking along them. Then the sound stopped outside her bedroom door. She presumed the wind must be causing the old house to creak and groan, and thought nothing of it at first as she buried her head under the bedding once more. And then a shiver ran down her spine as she heard the familiar words outside her door: "Are we having a cup of tea?"

Her heart pounded fiercely against the walls of her chest and she sat bolt upright in bed and listened.

"Are we having a cup of tea?"

She was unable to think clearly, she must be dreaming – yet she knew she was wide awake. But this was no dream. She knew she had heard that familiar voice repeating those tiresome, irritating words which had kept her awake, night after night, during her mother's wanderings. Each night her mother had climbed the stairs and walked along the floorboards which creaked with every footstep, before stopping outside the bedroom door and repeating those exact words.

"Are we having a cup of tea?" the frail voice whispered again. It was undeniably her mother.

The words were repeated over and over until finally Beryl got out of bed, the terror etched in her aged face. She hobbled over to the door, pinned her ear to it, and listened. She was afraid to open it, but she knew she must. She flung the door open and was greeted by the mewing of her old and failing cat, which was standing there looking bemused. Beryl shooed it away, angry that it had disturbed her, and angry that she had imagined something as ridiculous as her dead mother calling her as she once used to. She settled back down and it didn't take long for her to go back to sleep, once the palpitations had stopped. She let the incident steal away from her memory, and it was soon forgotten.

Several weeks later, Beryl awoke from a deep sleep to the sound of a melancholy tune being played on the old piano. She knew that tune well, as it was the one that Billy had first learnt to play as a young child. She recalled the many times he had played it for his mother, and how she had stood at his side marvelling at his musical talents which he had clearly inherited from her. Her senses were in turmoil, what was it, who was it? For a brief moment, albeit irrational, she thought Billy must have returned. He must be playing, he must have come back. She climbed stealthily off the bed, lit the candle, moved over to the door and opened it slowly. The music played louder and louder, until there was no mistaking that someone was down there. She hobbled down the stairs with great difficulty, her old bones creaking and groaning with pain. She crossed the dismal and dreary hall and looked hesitantly into the sitting room, but the music had stopped and no-one was there. She looked around, aided only by the dim light reflected by the candle. For a moment she was convinced that the music sheets had been moved from their normal place on the piano rest. But before she could make sense of it, she heard the sound of the rocking chair creaking as it moved back and forth on its old frame. Her heartbeat rose in volume as it thumped aggressively in her chest and seemed to echo in her ears. She headed apprehensively for the scullery, terrified of what she might see. But as she peered into the room she saw that the chair was empty – but it was rocking to a standstill as if someone had just got out of it. A shiver ran down her spine and the hairs on the back of her neck stood on end.

In the dim light of the flickering candle, everything looked sinister and unnerving. It was a big empty house for one person to be alone in, apart from the cat, and sounds had a tendency to echo in the night through the silence which penetrated the large empty spaces. There was only one answer, it was the cat that had been on the chair and had just jumped off. Probably the cat had been walking along the keys of the piano as well, and that was the sound she'd heard, not the familiar tune she remembered. Content with that explanation and convinced there was no-one else in the room apart from herself and the cat, she made her way back upstairs and into bed. She buried her head under the bedclothes and tried to settle, but once again she heard the eerie sound of the piano playing. This time she knew for certain that it was that same haunting tune which Billy had first learnt to play, and the sound seemed to magnify in the hollowness of the building. She began to tremble with fear, and shiver with cold at the same time, and her whole body began to shake from the aftermath, her bones aching with the strain. She buried herself more and more under the bedding in order to shut out the noise. But when the floorboards began to creak and stop right outside her door, she began to shake uncontrollably. Silence followed for one arduous minute after another. And then the horror began again.

"Are we having a cup of tea?" echoed the eerie voice; the sound gaining momentum as Beryl's heart-rate gained speed.

Convinced she was having a heart attack when a sharp pain tugged at her chest, she clutched at it in desperation. Her breathing was becoming difficult and she began to gasp for air. She rolled out of the makeshift bed and onto the floor, the cold penetrating her arthritic bones and causing unimaginable pain as she lay there in the darkness paralysed with fear and unable to move.

"Are we having a cup of tea?"

"Go away!" Beryl managed to call out, the pain in her chest becoming more severe and her breathing becoming more intolerable.

The cat screeched alarmingly from somewhere in the empty rooms on the top floor. She heard a door open and close, followed by a loud thud and then the creaking of the floorboards.

She was mortified!

The build-up of dread and anxiety in her mind, and the tension in her body made the pain more unbearable, and she had now come to the conclusion that these were her final moments. She was convinced that her mother had come to get her; a meeting she didn't want to have to face. But within a few seconds the sound of the music stopped, and at the same time her chest pains disappeared as well as the pain from her aching bones. Everything was silent until she heard her cat mewing outside the door. She dragged herself up from the floor and lit the candle. She waited for the flame to light up the room before going to the door and opening it fearfully. The cat was sitting there waiting patiently for her to let it in. Everything felt normal and there was neither sight nor sound of anyone else. She made her way downstairs and rejuvenated the dying embers of the fire so that she could make herself a cup of tea. She didn't feel like going back to bed, she'd had a terrible fright and one which would be hard to erase from her mind.

Several weeks passed by and there was no further unexplained activity going on in the house, and so Beryl soon settled back into her life of solitude. The incidents of that evening had been completely erased from her memory once more and she carried on as normal as if nothing had ever happened.

But it wasn't long before further events took over her mind, and her sanity was beginning to be questionable.

Beryl had gone to bed early because the evening had grown cold and her bones ached. She had taken a hot water bottle with her and wrapped her arms around it in bed, and soon she was sound asleep. But before long she was wakened from her slumber by the sound of haunting music. She lay there in the darkness listening to the mournful tune. The floorboards began to creak one by one, and she could hear the sound of doors opening and closing upstairs. Footsteps could be heard walking along the empty corridors, and the noises were amplified in the open spaces of the large and soulless house. Beryl clung onto the hot water bottle and hid under the bedclothes hoping she could blank out the sounds. Moments later the old, familiar voice spoke in a low, frail tone outside her door:

"Are we having a cup of tea?"

Beryl squealed in terror from under the bedclothes, and the noises from the top floor became louder as the voice repeated itself over and over again at her door:

"Are we having a cup of tea?" followed by shrieks of unnerving mirth which bounded along the landings and the hallway, and travelled through the large unoccupied rooms before disappearing into the distance.

Beryl's entire body became a shaking frame of pain-racked bones. And then, as if the horror wasn't great enough, she heard the sound of her bedroom door opening slowly. Her heart momentarily stopped, her throat muscles tightened, and her voice was non-existent as she tried to scream. Her breathing had become a series of rasps. She knew such intense fear could cause a heart attack, and so she prepared her mind for death once more as she writhed in pain and terror.

"Are we having a cup of tea?" the frail voice whispered above the bed.

"Go away!" Beryl managed to shriek back in utter desperation, too terrified to move as she gripped the bedding to stop her, or it, from pulling it away and exposing her to whatever purpose the demon had in mind.

"Are we having a cup of tea?" it cackled.

Beryl clutched the hot water bottle and slid further down the mattress, her body now in the foetus position as she sobbed in fright.

But life continued to cling on forcing her to witness whatever evil was to be bestowed on her, when immediate and sudden death would have been the desired choice. Her throat muscles, having suffered paralysis, ensured that even her panic-stricken gibberish was unable to be uttered. Now she knew how it would feel to be suffocated – or even throttled.

"Are we having a cup of tea?" The sound was relentless.

"Are we having a cup of tea?" followed by a sound of mirth as the voice trailed away out of the bedroom door and along the creaking floorboards. Loud laughter echoed through the building – mocking and taunting. It continued for what seemed to Beryl to be for hours, but in truth it lasted only a few moments. But in Beryl's mind her life was coming to a close, and she hoped against hope that it would be quick and so put an end to this slow tortuous punishment which she seemed doomed to have to endure.

And then the music stopped as suddenly as it had begun. The sounds from above died down and soon everything was silent. Only the emptiness of the building seemed to echo in her mind, but her fear wouldn't abate and she remained hidden under the bedding a shivering, shaking wreck. All that could be heard was the cat mewing outside her door. But nothing could entice her out of her place of refuge at the bottom of the bed, where she remained until she finally fell into a troubled sleep.

She awoke the next morning in the same position, with the dim recollection of the night's experiences slowly returning. She pulled herself to the surface and sat up in bed and could see the wintery sun shining in through the windows. She began to wonder if she'd perhaps had a nightmare. She dragged herself off the bed, walked over to the door, and opened it stealthily. She inspected the empty corridors and glanced down to the main hall. The sun streamed through and everything seemed to be deserted and quiet, but for the faint mewing of the cat. She concluded that she must have had a nightmare after all, as everything in the house seemed normal. She felt confident that it was safe to go downstairs.

But when the evening arrived Beryl couldn't brave the stairs. Her bones ached more than normal, which made her question if the previous evening's events had really happened and her aching bones were suffering from the aftermath. The fear of spending another night up there got the better of her, so she decided to keep a low fire in the grate of the range and sleep in the rocking chair. Wrapping her mother's old blanket around her she settled down for the night, but she had difficulty sleeping so she rocked the chair slowly in an attempt to soothe her bones and dull her senses. And for a while it worked. The burning embers of the fire cast a warm, but eerie glow in the small, cold scullery where no natural light could get in; but she soon felt comfy and warm as the blanket kept the draughts firmly at bay and she began to doze lightly.

But her peace was soon to be shattered. Whilst Beryl was in a semi-conscious state, the rocking chair was turned over abruptly and she fell hard onto the cold stone floor, bringing her harshly to her senses. She could hear the piano playing in the next room, and once again she was riddled with fear as she lay rigid on the floor. But when a warped mind is filled with terror an inner strength takes control, and so she managed to drag herself up. The sound of the music increased until it began to ring in her ears. She groped around in the dark until she found a small stub of a candle which she managed to light from the fire, whilst burning her hands in the process. She held it upright until the flame strengthened, before making her way to the sitting room where the sounds were coming from. But as she reached the doorway someone blew out the candle and Beryl shrieked in alarm. The cat mewed in front of her and she kicked it out of the way; it screeched as it disappeared from the room in a blind panic.

Beryl remained in one spot whilst she waited for her eyes to become accustomed to the dark, her body shaking in fear. The music sounded louder and the tune was clearly recognisable as the one that Billy had played for mother. She was riddled with horror at the thought of what she was about to witness. But as the darkness became lighter to her eyes, she was pushed to the floor from behind. She began to scream in terror as she struggled to drag her panic-stricken body off the floor; but when she finally got to her feet the music suddenly stopped. But to add to her alarm, doors were flinging themselves open and slamming shut again. Windows rattled and the sound of laughter ripped through the building. But it wasn't the normal sound of laughter it was a sinister, curdling sound which echoed hollowly throughout the house. But despite the change in tone, she instantly recognised the voice as that of her mother.

Without hesitation Beryl fumbled through the dark and headed for the front door. She slid the bolts open, turned the key in the lock and fled into the black night. Gaining unknown strength from somewhere, she ran into Gallows Lane and shrieked loudly. She headed for the old pub where a small light reflected from one of the windows, her senses to the pain of her arthritic bones numbed as the panic took control.

The barman saw a half-witted woman enter the room, her clothes in disarray and her grey, ragged hair standing on end. Her face was terror-stricken, her eyes wild and her speech garbled and senseless. An old man was standing at the corner of the bar across the room, and as he slowly sipped on his beer his faded blue eyes stared at her curiously.

The barman intuitively drew a whisky and placed it in front of her.

"Here drink that," he said calmly.

She drank it back and felt the liquid warm the back of her throat. It didn't take long for the effects of the drink to calm her down a little. Her hands were still shaking and the barman noticed her bent fingers, and instantly recognised the dreaded arthritis to be the culprit. The older man continued to sip at his beer as he stared at her, but he offered no solace.

"It's my mother," she managed to utter almost inaudibly. "She's come back – she's possessed the cat in order to haunt me. The cat has become a medium for her to communicate through."

Her voice gained momentum as her demeanour became more feverish. Even in her state of fright, she was sufficiently astute to push the glass towards the barman and motion for him to refill it; which he did while she continued with her crazed story.

He listened intently and so did the old man from across the bar. The barman displayed a show of sympathy towards the woman, but the old man felt no compassion, his face remained expressionless and impassive.

"She's trying to destroy me. She's paying me back for what I did to her and she's hell-bent on terrorising me until I drop dead. I know what she's up to she wants to lure me to where *she* is."

She drank the whisky more slowly this time before continuing.

"She's in hell," she hissed, her face contorting with venom. "Why can't she leave me in peace, my time will come soon enough. My punishment is in my bones, I suffer endlessly with the pain. She's evil and I know she won't stop until she's got me in her clutches. She's the devil, for sure she is."

She continued to babble uncontrollably, until the landlord finally lost his understanding of what she was saying. But it was clear to him that the woman had lost her mind. He ought to get in touch with the necessary authorities to take care of her, and maybe to-morrow he would do just that. In the meantime, he needed to get her back home and out of his pub. The old man seemed to be reading his mind, as he offered in a gruff voice to walk her back home.

"That's a good idea," he said to him with a nod, relieved that he wasn't going to have her in his bar ranting, and drinking free whisky for the rest of the evening.

The man walked round to her and told her to follow him, which she did. He instinctively led her up Gallows Lane and to Juniper House. He entered the grounds and walked through the open door in the porch. She followed quietly but hesitantly, as she pondered on his soft footsteps down the long hallway which she knew weren't loud enough to scare off any demons, or warn anyone of his presence. He walked across the main hall and into the sitting room, and stopped awhile as he surveyed the dilapidations which had taken control. His eyes lingered on the piano for a few moments before walking over to it. The dust and grime that clung possessively to the frame, and the keys, showed that no-one had used it for a very long time. He glanced at the mildewed music sheets and ran his fingers lightly across the keys, which allowed a sprinkling of dust to escape into the dank atmosphere.

"This hasn't been used for many years," he assured her quietly. "You must be mistaken when you thought you could hear music playing. It's plain to see that there's been no music in this house for a very long time."

He ventured into the scullery. The rocking chair, positioned in front of the range, was quiet and still. He pushed it lightly with his hand, but it would take much more than a gentle shove to make it rock. A blanket lay strewn upon the stone floor, and he picked it up and placed it carefully on the rocker. He wandered in and out of each room before going upstairs to each floor, inspecting all of the rooms as he went along. He noticed one door on the first floor had been blocked up, he knocked gently on it – it sounded hollow. But there was no sign of a ghost.

Once he had satisfied her that there was no presence in the house, he left her locking and bolting the door behind him. Once outside, he disturbed a cat in the garden which mewed as it disappeared behind the shrubbery. He wandered slowly back to the pub, and nothing more was mentioned about the incident.

The damage to Beryl's mind was long and calculated. She was beginning to look over her shoulder constantly, always fearing her mother's presence. But her mother remained silent week after each prolonged and punishing week. And her silence was beginning to affect Beryl, who was now starting to question her own sanity. She had no peace of mind, she was afraid of the dark, and her imagination was rampant. She found herself waiting for the next time.

And that time came soon enough.

As the evening beckoned, Beryl lit a candle and its soft glow cast shadows in the room which flickered in the gloominess of the night. Darkness soon took hold and the temperature began to drop throughout the empty spaces. Beryl took refuge in the small scullery where wood was still smouldering in the grate of the range. The back hall which contained the ancient pot sink was dark and chilled, and Beryl went in to ensure that the back door was bolted securely. Something prompted her to lift the candle up to the cracked mirror which was hanging on a hook above the sink, and as she looked into it she saw, to her horror, her mother's face grinning jubilantly back at her. She dropped the candle to the floor as she screamed in terror, and hobbled through the house as fast as her old legs would allow. She headed for the front door, stumbling in the dark as she attempted to find her way down the long hallway. She unbolted and unlocked the door and escaped screaming into the blackened night. She ran down Gallows Lane and through the hamlet, carrying on until she saw signs of life from other properties. She hammered on the doors of each house as she ran from one to another. Curtains opened and eyes peered out of the windows of each property, but quickly closed again at the sight of the mad woman tearing down the street. No-one came to her aid. She saw the dim light from the old pub ahead and ran towards it. She dashed in, screaming and ranting. The barman looked at her in trepidation, concerned that his few customers may leave at the daunting sight. He quickly moved towards her and sidled her round to where the old man was standing quietly at the corner of the bar. He looked at him for support, but none was forthcoming.

"Here, stand there and I'll get you a whisky," he instructed, almost pushing her at him regardless of his unwillingness.

He quickly pulled another beer for the man and drew a whisky for her. He placed them both on the bar. The man silently took his, but Beryl's demeanour was one of a dithering, shaking wreck and she couldn't stop her trembling hands long enough to pick up the glass.

"What's happened?" the barman asked. Although he suspected the woman was raving mad and had no doubt been hallucinating again.

"I've seen her ... in ...in the mirror," she stammered profusely. "She was laughing – laughing at me." She stared at him wildly.

The barman picked up the glass of whisky and clasped her hands round it.

"Here, drink it," he ordered.

She put the glass to her quivering lips and drank the liquid.

The barman could see she was in a state and was convinced that she shouldn't be living alone up the road in that great big house. The other man looked on coldly but said nothing, he carried on drinking.

"You really ought to have some company in that house. Have you no family?" asked the barman.

"No, no family. All dead," she replied. The back of her throat warmed to the drink and she felt her nerves calming.

"Not good for you to live alone in a place like that."

"No, no ... I don't want company. *She's* company enough," she replied frantically.

She drank the whisky back in one. The shock of the barman's remark had jolted her to her senses and she fled from the building in a blind panic. The last thing she wanted was interference from others, and she certainly didn't want him meddling in her affairs.

The barman nodded pleadingly to the old man, who quickly cottoned on as he reluctantly followed her outside. He walked up to the house with her in tow, and she offered no objections. She was comforted by his presence, he made her feel safe, although she couldn't fathom why. Maybe he was similar to her – solitary and reclusive.

She waited until he had gone into the house before following behind him. Once again he scoured the house for intruders, checking every room on every floor. He checked the security of the back door and all of the windows. Everything was rotting but still intact and fastened securely. He left the house after reassuring her that there was no presence, and she locked the door behind him.

She decided to make a hot cup of tea, so she put a pan of water on the range to boil. As she turned round, she found herself staring into the eyes of the cat which had been standing quietly behind her. But she knew those eyes, they were not the eyes of the cat at all, they belonged to her mother. She screamed in shock and horror, and kicked the cat all the way to the door. It shrieked as it fled from the house and into the grounds. Beryl locked the door and bolted it. She now had the answer to her problem. In order to get rid of her mother, she would need to get rid of the cat.

Soon after that last haunting the cat had gone and Beryl never saw her mother in Juniper again.

Several weeks had passed since the last incidents and Beryl had not set foot outside the house again, apart from collecting fuel from the old stores in the grounds. Life had taken on some normality for her, and she carried on her daily routine as if the recent past events had never happened. She slept more soundly in her bed, and the only disturbing noises to be heard during the night in Juniper House were from her snoring.

But one day as she dozed in the old rocking chair, the front door was broken down. Two men wearing white coats marched through the house and into the scullery where they saw the mad woman. They yanked her by the arms and dragged her screaming and kicking out of the door and into a waiting vehicle.

Beryl never saw Juniper House again. She spent the rest of her days in the York asylum where she had so cruelly arranged for her mother to be detained, after having had her sectioned in her master plan to gain everything for herself.

But it didn't end there for Beryl. Crazed with fear she often found herself being strangled into a straight-jacket and injected with drugs, as she put up a panic-stricken fight. But the most terrifying thing of all was when she looked into the face of the nurse who administered the drugs – she saw only her mother!

Juniper House was closed up and seized by the authorities as payment for the fees to keep Beryl locked away for the rest of her life.

There was no-one to mourn her death a few years later, when word had travelled to the small hamlet that she had finally died of madness. It came as no surprise and she was soon forgotten. She wasn't missed, she wasn't remembered, and no-one really cared. She'd ended her life as she'd lived it: a life without compassion, kindness, or consideration to others. Her parting had now suffered the same fate and lack of sentiment.

She was cremated and her ashes buried with those of her mother's inside the grounds of the asylum.

As one year after another slipped by, Juniper House was gradually forgotten by the residents of Judge Fields. Nothing major changed in the hamlet, life continued day after day, month after month, and year after year. Tall grasses and weeds from the long-neglected garden began to mount the old stone walls, keeping it hidden behind the trees and bushes and well away from the prying eyes of the outside world.

Although the authorities chose to offer the house for sale, it aroused little interest, until it was finally abandoned altogether. The marketing board which had been erected finally fell, and gradually over time it rotted into the ground. And as Gallows Lane didn't lead to anywhere except a narrow, winding, precarious road, which was difficult to access and which was treacherous in winter, it was hardly ever used. And so no-one ever learned of the existence of Juniper House and from then on it ceased to exist.

But inside strange things were happening, unexplained things, sinister and eerie, and no-one suspected. Somewhere in those empty spaces, faint stirrings of the past and its memories had been frozen in time and were relived in the still of night, undisturbed and undiscovered.

7

NOW

ANTON HAD BEEN TOLD by the local authority that his offer would be considered and they did not anticipate a problem. If things went according to plan, they expected the transaction to be completed by early the following year. They had even been told that the council could possibly arrange the finance. It was all too good to be true as far as Anton was concerned. He just knew that they were destined to become owners of Juniper House; it was fate that had taken them to the hamlet of Judge Fields that day – he just knew it. And to top it all, it was likely that they were going to get it at a bargain price if they accepted his ridiculously low offer.

He'd been told very little about the previous owners, except that the last two women had lived as recluses and had both gone mad. There were no other known family members. The house had been empty for many years, and as there was no-one personally responsible for its upkeep, it had deteriorated with time.

Lucy had had misgivings about the house from the very start, but she was even less impressed when she heard about the last two occupants having gone mad. Her mind continually reverted back to the old woman in ragged clothes, who she was convinced she had seen at the foot of the stairs that day. Maybe the old woman was one of the mad ones. But of course Anton thought *she* was mad for even suggesting it, and he was certainly not prepared to accept that she'd seen anyone and so refused to discuss it further.

But there was definitely something about that house and she just couldn't put her finger on it. All she knew was that she had reservations about the place and wished that Anton had never set eyes on it. He wouldn't listen to her, or see reason, which was so unlike him; and to crown it all he thought she was being neurotic and ungrateful.

He seemed to have gone through a personality change since the first time he'd seen Juniper. But that in turn made Lucy wonder whether she was now only just seeing the *real* Anton. Perhaps she'd been walking around wearing rose-tinted glasses and hadn't really been able to see through him – until now. She tried to push those terrible thoughts to the back of her mind otherwise she risked the two of them becoming distant.

But the nagging thoughts returned over and over again. Why was he so hooked on the place? She was mystified, and concerned too. But they had already set out on the road of purchasing the damned thing, and he wouldn't be deterred no matter what. Even if she refused to go along with it, he would still go ahead regardless and that hurt her deeply. So she had no choice but to stand by his side – or leave him. And the latter was not what she had in mind. However, the more she dwelt on it all, the more she came round to his way of thinking. Maybe he was right about her being typical of most women who walk around big, old, empty houses and become jittery; imagining that things will go bump in the night and the corridors will be haunted by previous occupants. Each time she approached the subject he was driven to laughter, making her feel rather dejected and silly. She decided to keep quiet in the end and not mention any of her speculative thoughts again.

During the time that Anton was the main key holder and whilst waiting for the loan to come through, he had been back to the pub a few times but it was never open. The old man seemed to have disappeared. He had hoped to see him again to thank him for his help and to buy him a beer, but every time he went over to Judge Fields to work on the grounds of Juniper, there was no sign of life.

He continually dwelt on the identity of the old man – the man with no name. Perhaps he was an ex-convict, guilty of some heinous crime for which he had served his sentence. His speech, Anton had noticed from the very beginning, had not been local but refined and he somehow had an air of superiority about him, plus an intelligence which was uncommon in a place like Judge Fields. His appearance contradicted his mannerisms and made Anton think he could be someone in disguise, someone who didn't want his identity known – maybe he was Lord Lucan. But he soon dismissed that because he didn't think he was old enough. He probably looked older than what he was, due to his stature and dishevelled appearance. The unshaven look and the long white hair may be part of his wish to remain incognito. Nonetheless, Anton was disappointed and sorry not to see him again. He presumed the pub was closed for the winter months because there was no point in opening, after all it did make sense as surely there wouldn't be sufficient customers out of season to keep it going. And with that thought in mind he looked forward to the turn of the season, in the hope that he would once more find him in there propping up the bar.

Anton continued to keep an eye on the house by spending his weekends there and clearing the gardens and bagging up rubbish. The authorities didn't care one way or the other what he did. Lucy stayed behind at their flat as she still had reservations about the house and its *occupant* and Anton couldn't understand her resistance and lack of enthusiasm. But undeterred he spent every minute of his leisure time there and the two of them hardly saw one other.

It was early February when the transaction was completed and they could call themselves the proud owners of Juniper House – at least Anton could do, Lucy wasn't so enthralled. He had promised her that the first thing he would do once they knew it was theirs was to change all the locks, hoping that way she wouldn't continue to harp on about another resident.

Lucy, meanwhile, had plenty to do at the flat to keep her mind occupied, such as packing and cleaning. They had a couple of months left on their lease, which would allow Anton some time to be getting the house habitable fairly quickly. He didn't mind roughing it, but he didn't feel it was fair to expect Lucy to do so. He took some holiday time which was due to him, having stored it up for when they would need it, and he worked day and night on the place. He had managed with great difficulty to get the electricity supply restored, which enabled him to get cracking on the internal work.

He did, however, have one guilty secret. Something had cropped up at work which meant he would have to be working away for a few weeks, as the job was long-distance. It meant leaving Lucy in the house alone for as long as the job took, and she wouldn't be too pleased about that. He deliberately kept it from her until the house was ready for them to move into, and even then he would have to pluck up some Dutch courage to break it to her. He brushed it aside knowing full well that he would have to face it sooner or later, but until then he didn't intend to worry about it.

8

THEY HAD HIRED A TRANSIT VAN to move their furniture. Anton wanted to do the house-move himself because they didn't have much money, and they had very little furniture seeing as how they'd lived in a very tiny flat. In fact it all looked rather pathetic once it was gathered together in the main hall. Lucy was feeling dejected because she didn't have Anton's foresight, she couldn't imagine how the house would look once all the work was finished, and it was just so vast. He tried to reassure her over and over again that it would be perfect by the time he'd done. Lucy wanted carpets, but there wasn't sufficient money left for such luxuries, so he planned to restore all the floorboards. Once sanded and stained, he promised, they would look great and a few rugs scattered around would add the finishing touches. Whilst Lucy was unconvinced she was happy to leave it in his capable hands – after all, he was always right in the end. Her design talents were restricted to the cosmetics and she had to trust Anton to have it all perfect in readiness for her input.

Anton had worked on one of the bedrooms for several weeks before the move. He had given it all a coat of paint and carried out any necessary repair work. The room he chose was the best in his opinion because it had two large windows which were all intact, therefore letting in lots of natural light; and it also had a large walk-in closet which would hold their clothes as well as additional storage. He had sanded and stained the floorboards and hung curtains and he was rather pleased with himself at the result.

So Lucy set to work on cleaning the bedroom in readiness for the evening. She wanted to make sure it was perfect before they moved their bed and other bits of furniture up there. Whilst she cleaned, Anton said he would carry their clothes up and hang them all neatly in the closet. They had bought a couple of rugs in readiness, which they both felt would look great once they were down.

"You forgot to move that old mattress out that's in here," she called to Anton as he mounted the stairs loaded with clothes. Her voice seemed to echo in the large empty spaces.

"Oh sorry love, I'd forgotten about that. It won't take a minute cos it's so worn out that the weight has all gone out of it, so I can manage it on my own." He started to put the clothes in the closet. "I'll have to do something about those creaking floorboards on the landing I've never heard anything as bad before. If you hear those creaking in the night you'll be thinking we've got intruders."

"Well how could they creak during the night if we're in bed asleep? They're only likely to creak if we walk on them." She didn't know whether to feel unnerved by what he'd just said. She hadn't thought of them creaking whilst they were sleeping, and she didn't much like the idea now he'd mentioned it, it was likely to set off her imagination again.

"Wouldn't we be better leaving them as they are then, so we'll know if someone is walking on them when we're asleep?" Her mind was working overtime and she was feeling jittery at the thought. She'd never lived in a house so big in her life, and all the empty rooms didn't do much to make her feel secure. She was rather wishing he hadn't come out with that last remark.

"I wasn't thinking straight love, I'm just being silly. Of course no-one will be walking on them when we're asleep – unless we have guests, so don't fill your head with that kind of nonsense."

The subject wasn't mentioned again.

They both carried their bed and mattress upstairs. The wide curved staircase made it so much easier than a normal one. Anton took the old mattress outside and threw it in the van, while Lucy began to add the finishing touches to the bedroom with some new crisp bedding which they had bought as a special treat. She placed two table lamps on the bedside cabinets and after adding the two rugs and some other odds and ends, she had to admit it was looking cosy and inviting and she couldn't wait to try it out. The lamps gave the room a soft glow once she'd closed the curtains, and she looked around to admire the finished result.

Anton also gave it his seal of approval before the two of them went downstairs to make a cup of tea. He had already lit the fire in the sitting room and the one in the Yorkshire range, and soon the heat flowed evenly throughout the living area and the scullery.

"We can use the range for cooking until I build a kitchen, then you can have a proper cooker as well. But I'm rather looking forward to using this," Anton said excitedly as he poked around at the wood to stir some life into it.

Lucy could see he had worked hard at cleaning the range. The jet black shone so much you could almost see your face in it, and there was a pan of water simmering gently on the stove.

"Here sit in this old rocker whie I make you a drink." He beckoned her over as he moved it closer to the fire.

She did as she was instructed because she was feeling exhausted, and more than a little hungry.

After raiding their food stock, Anton returned with a cup of tea and a pan containing soup. He handed the tea to Lucy and placed the pan of soup on the range to warm. He retrieved their foldup table from the hall, which they normally used in their camper van, and moved it towards her. He then brought in some bread, butter, cutlery and condiments and got organised at making them something to eat.

"Fresh bread and butter and soup, it's just like being in the camper," he said enthusiastically.

Lucy could see he was really excited by the whole experience, and she left him to it whilst she closed her eyes and sat back in the rocker. But she had the strangest experience when her eyes were closed. She saw an old woman – in fact it was the same old woman who she had first seen at the foot of the stairs, she was certain of it. She saw her standing in front of her, glaring at her as she rocked the chair gently. She opened her eyes swiftly, but of course there was no-one there. All she could see was the pleasant glow of the fire and Anton rustling up some grub. She blinked her eyes and closed them again. But after a minute or two, she saw the image once more and this time it seemed even more real. It made her feel restless and uncomfortable, as if she shouldn't be in the old rocker at all, so she stood up.

"What's wrong?" Anton asked.

"It's not very comfy," she fibbed.

"No probs, I'll get you a proper chair to sit on."

He went to retrieve a chair from the hall and brought it back for Lucy to use. She placed it a safe distance away from the rocker, as she didn't want to take any chances. The old woman's face had haunted her from the start, and sitting in that chair had brought it all back. She didn't know if she'd imagined it or not, but the experience had left her somewhat perturbed.

Later that evening they were both thoroughly bushed, but at least they could sit in front of the fire in the sitting room and relax. Anton had done his best to make it as comfortable as possible, although it was just a temporary arrangement. They had the range to cook on in the scullery and the room had to also double up as a kitchen, along with the back hall containing the pot sink. As for their kitchen appliances, they had to be positioned in various parts of the sitting room wherever they could find a power point. Fitting additional ones was on Anton's priority list, but it would all take time. Although there wasn't a real kitchen as such – no work surfaces or cupboards – there was an old pantry which they would be able to use once it was cleaned and decorated, and they could manage quite well with their old kitchen table to work and sit at for the time being. After a summer season touring around in a camper van, they were able to adapt with ease at their new surroundings and they looked on it all as an adventure. Anton knew it would take a very long time to wade his way through the entire house; it was big and rambling and had three floors, and although it was a daunting task he was determined.

They retired to bed early as the house was getting chilled, and they were too exhausted to do anything else having been hard at it all day after a very early start. At least the bedroom was cosy and inviting and they were both snug and warm in bed, so much so that they both fell sound asleep within minutes.

But Lucy awoke with the sound of Anton snoring, so she pushed him hard to roll him over to face the other side; at least if he started again it wouldn't be in her ear. She got comfy once more and was soon fast asleep. But she was soon awakened again by the sound of snoring. She sat up in bed and could see that Anton hadn't moved since she'd shoved him over. But whilst she could hear snoring, it clearly wasn't coming from him. She sat in the same position for a while in complete confusion. How could she hear snoring if it wasn't coming from Anton? She had no answer. But once she concentrated and listened carefully, she realised the snoring sound was coming from the floor and directly beneath where she was sitting. But how could that be? She was perplexed. Leaning over the side of the bed, she stuck her head underneath whilst clinging onto the mattress, but then she began to slide slowly down the bed and had to cling on tighter. At that point Anton woke up and turned his head towards her

"What are you doing?" he asked, rubbing his eyes as if he were seeing things. He sleepily eyeballed her bottom which was sticking up in the air.

Lucy almost fell off the bed as she struggled to get back up again, so Anton grabbed her by her nightie and dragged her back onto the bed.

The snoring had stopped, so she knew she was going to look rather foolish.

"I heard snoring – it was coming from the floor underneath the bed."

Anton groaned, grabbed the bedding and swiftly turned over burying himself under the duvet. Within minutes he had resumed his sleep and was snoring, and there was no mistaking this time where the sound was coming from.

Lucy wasn't too happy about the experience. She shivered, but it was more from a feeling of eeriness than cold. She was certain that snoring was coming from the floor underneath the bed. She turned towards Anton pulling herself as close to him as possible, before burying her head under the bedding. Fortunately she had muffled out any chance of further noises and soon fell asleep.

Anton awoke early the next morning and turned to face Lucy, but she wasn't there. He sat up and looked around the room, but there was no sign of her. *Perhaps she's got up early to make a brew and something to eat,* he hoped. So he jumped out of bed and opened the bedroom door.

"Luce!" he called, his words echoing down the empty staircase.

"What do you want?" was the muffled reply.

He spun round to see her legs and feet sticking out from under the bed. She slid herself back out, stood up and brushed herself down in the process.

"What are you doing?" he exclaimed, looking puzzled.

"I was looking to see where that snoring noise came from."

Anton looked at her in exasperation, threw his arms up in the air and gasped. He marched round to the bed, pulled on some clothes which he had, unusually, left on the floor the night before, and disappeared out of the room.

Lucy got dressed and tidied up the bed, before following meekly down the stairs. When she walked into the scullery she found he had retrieved their electric kettle and he was now boiling water and preparing bacon for frying on the range. He had made sure it was packed with fuel the previous evening in order for it to stay in all night in readiness for breakfast. She knew he was annoyed with her about the snoring sounds, after all, it did sound pretty stupid in the cold light of day. She'd probably imagined it as usual anyway. She knew the best thing to do was to get on with helping him to make breakfast and keep quiet – he'd snap out of his little tantrum!

By the time they sat down to eat their food – which by now was on the dining table in the sitting room – he had forgotten all about the incident and was back to his cheery self. He wasn't one for sulking, or getting angry, he had a calming influence on Lucy because he was so laid back about everything and nothing ever presented a problem to him. There wasn't anything he could not tackle, or sort. She could understand him getting a little bit frustrated with her after all the hours he had put in to get the house ready for habitation, she couldn't blame him for that. She couldn't help but think how she loved his orderliness, his organised methods and eagerness to get everything as perfect as possible. He had surprised her that morning by organising the table and chairs at the back of the sitting room so they could have a proper dining area; it was just like him to do that and she loved him for it. She was a bit of a scatterbrain herself, but she did try to be more organised so that she wouldn't let Anton down.

They ate in silence and although the house was virtually empty and needed a complete overhaul, the scullery and sitting room glowed warmly from the heat of the fire and the range, plus the cosy atmosphere which they had managed to create with their joint efforts.

"Oh, I see you've moved the old rocker," she interjected as an afterthought.

"Yes, I've decided I'm going to use it, if you don't find it comfy enough. I thought it was quite comfortable when I tried it, especially with that old cushion on it which I found in a cupboard. It's so old that rocker that I would suspect it could tell a tale or two. It's one of those things you'd sit on in front of the fire on a cold winter's night telling ghost stories. I think you should wash that old blanket Luce, the one which was on the floor, it's ideal for wrapping round the legs whilst rocking. I love old things like that, it's very nostalgic. My old granddad had one very similar and I used to sit on his knee as a child when he was on it. He would rock away whilst I cuddled up to him. Ah yes, fond memories, I remember it all so well!" He sighed deeply, as his reminiscing brought back happy thoughts of his childhood. "So, I've decided that I'm going to keep it and the old cushion and blanket as well. I think I'll leave it there where it is at the side of the fireplace."

Lucy couldn't help but think the old cushion and the drab, grey, woollen blanket were past their sell-by-date, and she wasn't much keen on washing them either. Who knows where they'd come from, or what they'd been used for; she cringed at the thought.

Her thoughts turned to Anton. It was evident that he was turning into a slightly unrecognisable and over-contented human being. His lust for excitement and adventure seemed to have disappeared, having been replaced with Juniper; and that's all he seemed to need now. She frowned as she watched his smug expression of satisfaction. Clearly *he* wasn't being visited by some peculiar old woman in rags when he sat on the old rocker. Lucy felt strangely demoralised. Was there some kind of bizarre conspiracy going on here, which was beyond her understanding? The whole scenario was certainly questionable.

He continued to scoff his food, and gave a sigh of approval when he'd finished. There was no doubt he was as pleased as punch in his new surroundings and was enjoying the simple basic lifestyle which they were currently stuck with, at least for now. He was king of the castle in his own little fantasy world, and Lucy felt as if they'd suddenly turned into a pair of old, married pensioners, and the two fun-loving young people that they used to be before Juniper had ceased to exist.

"It may sound strange, but I feel as if I've finally come home."

"This is home," she reminded him, while at the same time reflecting on what she'd just said and wondering if she could ever think of it as *home*.

"I know, but it's more than that. I feel as if I've just returned from a very long voyage and I belong here. It's as if this has always been home for me. It has that kind of welcoming feel, one that recognises you as if you're a past friend." He sat back in his chair with a look of self-satisfaction on his face, having just had his belly full and looking quite content. Lucy couldn't help but think he was behaving as if he were 'lord of the manor', not mortgagee of an old decrepit house – and with a huge debt round both of their necks.

She could see that Juniper had really got under his skin and she was beginning to feel as if she didn't belong in his fantasy world any more, as if this house was all about *him*. In fact, he was making her feel like an intruder – or the charwoman, and she wasn't certain which category she most fitted into. But the constant nagging thoughts remained firmly fixed in her mind, that whilst *he* was being welcomed home – as he put it – *she* was being made to feel like an outsider, or maybe even an obstacle! She couldn't put her finger on it, but she certainly felt no sense of belonging and she couldn't help but wonder if she could ever truly settle.

9

As the days passed Anton worked his way through the house from morning until night, while Lucy scrubbed and cleaned and cooked – having eventually got the hang of the range. She soon found herself enjoying their new home, or at least part of it. The finished parts had taken on a reasonably friendly atmosphere, once they had begun to put their own stamp on it, but there was still a long way to go. Lucy began to wonder if perhaps she had been acting rather foolishly lately by insisting that she'd seen that old woman, and complaining of snoring sounds in the bedroom – not to mention her petulant behaviour with some silly notion that she was having her nose pushed out. She had to admit to herself that she'd been sounding rather neurotic lately, and that could easily build a bridge between them if she didn't pull herself together. Anton had gone out of his way to push ahead with the house purchase and work extremely hard at creating a home for her. Any woman would give her right arm for a man like him, and right now she was suffering from a guilty conscience.

Anton had plumbed the washing machine in and together they were quite organised. Although the house looked sparse and drab elsewhere, the sitting room and the scullery looked and felt more homely, and even inviting to a certain extent. Fortunately with Anton having worked hard on the gardens and grounds whilst waiting for the mortgage to come through, it was all looking good outside and soon they were both proud to say they were the owners of Juniper House.

Days turned into weeks, and the time was growing close to when Anton would have to tell Lucy that he would be working away. He wasn't looking forward to it, particularly as she had been in good form lately showing signs of enjoying their new home and paying him a lot of attention – just like she always used to do. He'd been feeling pretty good about that. They'd been going to bed early and getting close, and she seemed to have lost all her superstitions about the house having a presence – or two.

At least he'd managed to finish decorating the most important rooms, which were the sitting room and the scullery, plus the back hall with the pot sink in it, and a few more parts here and there. There was no doubt he was being somewhat over-sentimental when he'd put the old cracked mirror back on the hook above the sink, especially when Lucy had earmarked it for binning. But it was there when they moved in, and somehow he felt that it rightfully belonged there.

In general it looked much more enticing – and not quite as spooky, as Lucy had been quick to point out. However, the long hallway from the entrance door to the grand hall, plus the staircase and landing, were gloomy, shabby, dilapidated and darkly lit – not to mention the second floor which was uninhabitable! He was able to see through the dilapidations up there and imagine how it would look once all the work was done. But he knew Lucy would never venture up onto that floor in a thousand years, so there was no urgency to start on that area, and there were still plenty of rooms downstairs to make a start on. It was a pretty big house with six bedrooms on the first floor, plus more rooms could be found via the secondary staircase leading to the second floor, which probably once served as the nursery and staff rooms. Anyway, as far as he was concerned, the parts which mattered to Lucy the most were looking ship-shape for when he was gone. Surely she wouldn't mind him working away after all the efforts he'd put in, and, after all, it was for her benefit. However, he still kept putting it off until he knew he couldn't put it off any longer.

"Lucy love," he began.

Lucy was immediately alerted to something fishy going on. He didn't call her by her proper name unless he was sheepish about something. She walked over to him and eyed him suspiciously.

His courage failed him when he observed her with her hands on her hips. He pretended to be looking elsewhere, nonchalantly tidying up here and there.

"What are you up to?" she quizzed bluntly.

"Err ... well – you know that lovely bathroom suite you saw ... and the shower cubicle?" He squirmed as he edged his way around the truth of the matter.

"What about it?" she asked sternly. She was no fool when it came to Anton looking sheepish.

"Hum – I'm going to do some overtime so I can get it for you. I can do all the work myself, so it isn't out of reach pricewise." He spat it out so quick that he didn't fool her for one minute.

"And what exactly do you mean by overtime?"

He shuffled around feeling uncomfortable, and he couldn't look her in the face. But he knew he had to come clean, so best to get it over with.

"I'll be working in Somerset for a few weeks."

"Well that's what you think!" she snapped.

"Sorry love, but it is part of my contract. I know how much you want a nice new bathroom, rather than that old cast-iron one up there. And to be honest I think I should earn enough to be able to get the materials for the kitchen as well, which I want to build for you. You'd like that Luce, really you would. You know you don't like having to work between the scullery and the sitting room, and it's the only way we're going to get what we want. We can't live like this forever."

He was guilty of bribery tactics and he knew it, but he'd had to pull something out of the hat quickly before an explosion erupted.

She came down off her high horse once the reality of what he was saying began to sink in.

"But what will *I* do?" she whimpered. "I don't want to be here alone at night." In fact she shuddered at the thought. "I've never lived on my own before."

"But you won't be living on your own will you? I'll be coming back again. It's only going to be for a few weeks."

"Only a few weeks?" she gasped in alarm.

"Well, maybe only three..." He broke off as his courage failed him again and he couldn't bring himself to admit to the likelihood of it being much longer.

"But I can't stay here alone for three weeks!"

"You'll be alright love, there's nothing to be afraid of, and it's only until the job's done. Maybe it won't take so long, and then when I come back we can go and choose the bathroom and kitchen." He put a reassuring arm around her shoulders and hugged her to him, but she quickly pulled herself loose.

"It may not seem long to you – you're not the one who'll be staying here alone. It sounds like a life sentence to me and I don't think I can do it," she moaned pathetically.

She was beginning to panic internally. Her mind began to wander back to the things that she had tried so hard to push behind her: the old woman, the snoring, and the sheer creepiness of some parts of the house – in fact most parts of the house. It didn't bear thinking about.

Suddenly they were all becoming real again and her imagination was beginning to take over once more.

"I'll make sure everything is secure before I go. By the time I've finished you'll wonder what all the fuss was about."

Lucy had never imagined that she would have to consider sleeping alone in the house, she was only just adjusting to actually living in it – and even that was touch and go.

She had to concede that this was one debate she was definitely going to lose. And whilst she was far from pleased, she knew she couldn't do a thing about it. Maybe if she focused on the idea of a new bathroom and kitchen, it would distract her from the fear of sleeping alone at night in a house which was far too big for a couple, let alone one person – and to make matters worse, a house which would scare the living daylights out of any normal person.

She really did want a new kitchen, there wasn't one as such, and as for the bathroom it was really grotty. She had tried everything possible to clean the toilet, but nothing worked and she really hated having to use it. So there were plenty of reasons to feel happy at Anton's plans – but being alone in that big empty house was not one of them. In fact, the mere thought of it scared her half to death. She knew she would now spend every minute, of every day, leading up to when he was due to leave, living in sheer terror at the idea.

The dreaded day came too quickly and it was upon them before Lucy had time to adapt her mind to it. She had packed Anton's clothes and toiletries in the van the night before he was due to set off. By the following morning she had butterflies in her stomach and she was wondering how on earth she was going to cope without him.

Sensing her fear and anxiety from the outset, Anton had installed some external security lights for her, which was a help, although Lucy wondered if they would make matters worse. What if, for example, the lights came on outside due to the wind, or perhaps even a stray cat? After all, they were sensitive to any movement catching the beam, so it could easily happen. And if it did, she would have good reason to suspect intruders were trying to get in. So she would have preferred a straightforward external lamp which could be manually operated by a switch inside the front door, so that she could leave it on all night. But Anton insisted he knew what he was doing. He had also installed a make-shift alarm, but once again Lucy thought that could be a problem if it went off and turned out to be a false alarm – what would THAT do to her? And anyway, it wasn't outside intruders that she was worried about, that wasn't her main concern. It was whatever lurked indoors that made her afraid. Once he was gone, she would be vulnerable on her own to whatever sinister presence might be lying in wait for her – for example, that old woman! And who knows, she may even have accomplices.

She had really tried to drum some sense into her head. She'd tried to brainwash herself into believing that there was no such thing as a ghost, and haunted houses didn't really exist if that's what was worrying her. But it wasn't working. She was becoming seriously imaginative, and by the time he was due to leave – she was a dithering wreck.

"All you have to do love is to leave some lights on as soon as it starts to darken. A lamp down here and one in the hall and the ones in our bedroom will make you feel safer. You'll be alright, just wait and see," he reassured her again. "If you take your mind off all the empty parts of the house, they'll soon cease to exist and you'll wonder why you ever made such a fuss." But funny enough, it wasn't working.

"Putting lights on in the hall makes it look creepier than ever," she mumbled as a pout forced its way through.

"But you'll get used to it, honest you will. It's only because there isn't any wallpaper on the walls, and it's all darkened with age." He held her by the shoulders and looked at her confidently. "It's *our* home now, our little nest. Think of it like that. It's true what they say you know, that beauty is in the eye of the beholder – and so is fear. It's all part of your imagination which causes you to believe that things are happening just because you're alone. But think about it, why would something happen because I'm not here, if it doesn't happen when I am?" He gave her a quick peck on the forehead.

Lucy looked at him in bemusement. *It's alright for him being brave, but he's not the one staying behind.* So his logic couldn't penetrate her mind – he hadn't left yet and she was already feeling quite sick.

"Why can't I come with you?" she pleaded.

"Aw, you know you can't love. I'm going to work – it's not a holiday. What would you do each day and who would look after the house? And anyway, we need the money."

"I could stay in the van. I could have your meals ready each day, just like I normally do." She was beginning to feel frantic.

But Anton just smiled and shrugged it off. He knew she would eventually settle down to the idea – she had no choice. She was just behaving like any other woman who was faced with the same predicament; they always get scared when they're alone in the dark. It's just the way it is.

And so it was left like that.

Anton set off early and Lucy was alone in the house for the first time. She was glad of her part-time job to go to otherwise she would have felt extremely lonely by herself day and night. It was only a short walk to the bus stop that would take her to work and she had become quite used to it, but she had to make sure she arrived at the bus stop in good time as there wasn't another bus for three hours; such was the hamlet of Judge Fields.

He had promised to drive back up North to be with her each weekend, so she felt much better about that, and her little job would help to kill some time. She would be out in a morning and by the time she did some shopping and caught the bus back home, it would be midafternoon. She would spend the rest of her time cleaning and sorting out some more of their belongings, and by the time she had cooked something to eat it would be bedtime. Hopefully the days and nights would pass quickly, but even though she'd tried to convince herself of that, somehow it didn't seem to penetrate her mind sufficiently for her to feel better. It's just that the days were not a problem – the nights were!

When she got home that day it was four o'clock. She had offered to work some extra hours and that had helped to utilise some time before popping to the shops for something for tea. When she got through the door it felt empty and lonely. She hadn't realised just how quiet it was until now, apart from the sound of her footsteps echoing loudly on the bare floorboards. She walked across the main hall – which now seemed even more shabby and dilapidated – and as she walked into the sitting room and across to the scullery, she stopped suddenly. She had just walked past the old cushion and it was on the floor; it was the one that Anton used on the old rocker. And what's more, the rocker had gone! She stopped and stared in bemusement as she picked up the cushion. She walked into the scullery and to her surprise found the rocker back in its former place in front of the old range. She stared at it in amazement, her mind momentarily blank. She was certain it was in the sitting room, where Anton had left it, before she went to work. She certainly couldn't recall him moving it back in front of the range. Perhaps he'd moved it back and she just hadn't noticed. But it wasn't like Anton to throw the cushion on the floor – *she* might just do that, but he definitely wouldn't.

She wasn't short of ideas to fuel her imagination, so she could do without any strange happenings during the time she was out at work – and whilst Anton was away. But no matter how hard she tried to convince herself that the cushion must have accidentally been dropped that morning when Anton moved the rocker into the scullery, the more she doubted it. She knew Anton, he was a stickler for tidiness and organisation, which held her in check too because by nature she was just the opposite – or had been until she'd met him. So if Anton had been moving the rocker, which she still doubted, and the cushion had dropped on the floor, he would've picked it up – she knew he would. Or perhaps he just hadn't seen it because his mind was too busy worrying about leaving her on her own? After all, no-one is infallible – couldn't he just for once have made a mistake?

But her mental wanderings just wouldn't let her be, because there was the matter of that old woman again and that rocker. Her imagination was being tried and tested to its limit, and Anton would definitely think she was going slightly mad if he knew. It was bad enough telling him about the old woman she had seen in the first place, he'd never quite let her live that down. Then came the snoring lark – he definitely wasn't amused by that. If she attempted to mention the old rocker having moved by itself into the scullery – well, she wouldn't care to think what his reaction would be. But she was still certain it wasn't there when she'd left that morning. Maybe she *was* going slightly bonkers. Thoughts of madness brought back the memory of what Anton had been told by the local authority. Hadn't he said that the last two occupants had been driven mad? What if the same thing was happening to her? Could that old adage: *everything happens in threes*, be true? Could she be number three occupant who would be driven insane? It didn't bear thinking about. Then her nervous thoughts turned into angry ones. She'd always known there was something strange and sinister about the house. She'd felt it from the first time she'd peered through that dirty old pane of glass and seen some peculiar old woman staring back at her. And why should it be presumed that it was *her* feeble imagination? Why could she not be given the benefit of the doubt and presume that there *was* really someone at the bottom of the stairs at the time? After all, the pub landlord and the old man had certainly reacted when she'd asked them who she was. And there was something rather strange about that old man too – after all, why had he suddenly disappeared after palming the keys off to a naïve and gullible Anton?

In fact there was something fishy about the whole thing!

There was no doubt in her mind that Anton was becoming possessed by the house, or something in it, which was much more disturbing than his obsession on first seeing it. Because being obsessed by it, and being possessed by it, were two entirely different things and somehow it was taking him over, she was sure of it. He wasn't quite the same old Anton she knew – it was as if he was becoming someone else. And the more he seemed to get sucked in, the more, it seemed, that she was being pushed out and she didn't know why. Was it a ploy to get rid of her so that the house could have him all to itself? But now her mind was rambling incoherently and she was bordering on becoming neurotic. If she didn't watch herself the house might possess her too, but not exactly in the same way as it seemed to want to possess Anton. Did something sinister want to possess her mind? It didn't bear thinking about, because surely that route could only lead to the asylum, which would be to follow in the footsteps of the previous occupants. She shuddered at the idea.

She desperately needed to drive the nonsense out of her head and pull herself together otherwise Anton wouldn't be the only one to think she was mad. There were only two options as far as she was concerned, either she was right, or she was wrong. Maybe time would prove it one way or another.

She walked determinedly towards the old rocker and dropped the cushion onto the seat with a vengeance, and then immediately stepped back from it again. She didn't even dare touch it, let alone move it back into the sitting room. What was it about that stupid old rocker that could have such an effect on her? She had a mind to throw it in the skip which was out in the garden. And the more she allowed herself to dwell on that idea, the more she was tempted to do so. She could do it whilst Anton was away, but what would he say when he returned? After all, he had become rather attached to it. And she knew he would never forgive her, so the idea was more than her life was worth. So she had no choice but to leave it where it was, and where it evidently wanted to be. She kept a wide berth each time she had to pass it, and eyed it suspiciously when doing so. It might be just an old rocker, but strange things had happened to her each time she got too close to it. Better not to think about it again, otherwise she risked becoming paranoid.

She already had too many unanswered questions in her mind, to which she preferred not to seek answers. She was nervous enough at the thought of being left alone in a house which was becoming increasingly more difficult for her to call home, without looking for additional excuses to become a raving lunatic. If her earlier thoughts were right and Juniper didn't want her there, and for some unfathomable reason it wanted Anton, then surely she should be strong and not let it get the better of her. And anyway Anton belonged to her, why should she give him up without a fight, after all she found him first. But she stopped herself from going any further with her bizarre notions, otherwise she risked falling victim to the wayward and melodramatic thoughts of a phobic woman. And wasn't it a bad idea to be concentrating on such disturbing thoughts when she had to sleep alone in the place for the very first time – and in just a few hours? She was already feeling jittery and had butterflies in her stomach as she dreaded the oncoming evening. She really did need to get her act together and come to her senses otherwise she wouldn't last the night on her own.

Soon the darkness of the evening began to cast its eerie shadow around Juniper and Lucy began to feel the first serious signs of unease. She had heeded Anton's advice and switched on some lamps, and she'd also dug out a couple more from the unpacked boxes in the hall. Although there were no spare shades for them, at least they would give some extra light and they were better than nothing. She plugged one in to an old socket which she'd spotted in the main hall, but when she switched it on the vast hall and staircase took on an even spookier and more eerie atmosphere. On reflection, it was better left in the dark so she couldn't see it. She felt an involuntary shiver run down her spine as she wondered whether she should unplug it again. However, she chose to leave it where it was hoping she'd get used to it. Having found an extension lead in Anton's box of tools and paraphernalia, she plugged the second one into a socket in the sitting room; it helped a little and it was the best she could do, and as she wasn't planning on staying downstairs any longer than need be, it hardly mattered. She intended to leave them all on through the night, as Anton had suggested, so she wouldn't feel so nervous.

She decided to leave the two bedroom lamps switched on and close the curtains early so that it would look welcoming and warm when going to bed. She'd also found an old hot water bottle in an empty cupboard in the scullery, and checked it for punctures before filling it up. She placed it in the bed early on in the evening with her nightdress wrapped firmly round it. At least it would be nice and warm before she got in later. Thankfully the atmosphere of the bedroom felt different to the rest of the house, and she was certain that she'd feel less nervous once she'd shut herself in there for the night.

Anton had left her with sufficient fuel for the sitting room fire and the range. He had stacked up large quantities of wood in the porch, as well as in boxes in the scullery. He'd shown her how to bank up the fires so that they would still be in the following day. So having followed his instructions she was quite happy that her organisational skills were taking on a new dimension.

At eight o'clock that evening she decided to go to bed, so she prepared herself a hot drink to take with her and a book to read. As she walked through the dismal hall and mounted the stairs, she couldn't help but feel increasingly nervous. It had been touch and go all day, ever since she arrived home. The spooky atmosphere of walking into an empty house alone had already given her palpitations, and it had taken all the courage she possessed to face the oncoming apprehensions of being alone. But surely if she got through the first day and night, the rest would be easier. Or could that be wishful thinking?

She rushed into the bedroom and slammed the door shut behind her. She immediately locked it with the small bolt that Anton had fitted for her in order to help her feel more safe and secure, and it worked to a certain extent. She got undressed, donned her nice warm nightie and climbed into bed. She propped up the pillows having used Anton's to give her extra support, and breathed a sigh of relief that she'd got so far. She was hoping that by reading a book she was less likely to imagine noises, and anything else which could possibly spook her. It was important not to allow her imagination to be fuelled by the fact she was now truly alone in a house which, in its present condition, would freak out the most ardent of sceptics. She closed her mind to the empty rooms above and hoped that she wouldn't hear a single sound from any of them.

She settled down at nine o'clock hoping to get a good night's sleep. She was drowsy and feeling reasonably relaxed, so once she was asleep she would be dead to the world – at least that's what she was hoping. She repositioned the pillows, put her book away, and slid under the duvet. She slipped her arm around Anton's pillow and snuggled into it, and with the lamps left on she felt quite comfortable and safe – for the time being.

She was just drifting into a slumber when she thought she'd heard the floorboards creaking. It sounded as if someone was walking on them, and she very quickly re-entered the land of the living. Her eyes flicked open, and she stopped breathing in order to silence the excessive thumping in her chest which she felt certain could be heard by any potential intruder. She gripped Anton's pillow evermore tightly and listened. The creaking stopped right outside her door. She felt that she was going to be physically sick, and she struggled to breathe because her terror was so intense.

"Are we having a cup of tea?" a frail but sinister voice called outside the door.

Her body seemed to go into paralysis mode and she couldn't move. She tried to tell herself that it wasn't really happening, that she was in a doze and had only *thought* she'd heard it. Maybe she was having a nightmare. Maybe she would wake up properly soon and breathe a sigh of relief on finding it was just a bad dream. But deep down she knew she was kidding herself in the hope that the horrible sound wouldn't come again. She waited for what seemed like an eternity, as she continued to clutch at the pillow. She allowed only sporadic moments in which to shallowly breathe, for fear of the sound exposing her whereabouts under the bedding. She waited and waited as time seemed to stand still, and even her thoughts weren't allowed to interrupt the silence. But she eventually relaxed her breathing once sufficient time had passed to convince her that she hadn't heard anything after all.

But the gruesome reality came to fruition when she heard the dreaded sound again.

"Are we having a cup of tea?"

There was no mistaking it this time and all her wishful thinking and hopes of discovering it was all in her mind, brought on by a nightmare, were eliminated in that split second. The brutal truth that someone, or something, was outside her bedroom door hit her hard, and her fear was exacerbated knowing she was alone in the room with no-one to cling to and no hope of escape.

She almost shrieked out loud but as quickly as the sound tried to exhale from her quaking body she pulled it back in again, as she tried desperately to keep quiet in the hope that whatever was outside her door might go away if she remained silent.

But in those few excruciating moments, her reasoning burst into action and reminded her that it obviously knew she was there or it wouldn't be hovering outside her door.

She crawled under the duvet and began to cry in terror, burying her face in the pillow to try to muffle her sobs. She was so petrified that even her brain seemed to have shut down.

"Are we having a cup of tea?" the voice called again, but this time it was more threatening.

But worse was to come. Within seconds, to her horror, she heard the door handle turn as the perpetrator tried to get in.

Lucy was so horrified that her reasoning seemed to have frozen, leaving her in a state of limbo as if in a trance. She lay there helpless and desperate in a state of complete shutdown. She was unable to imagine ever seeing the light of day again, because surely these were her final moments as nothing stood in the way of whatever was outside that door.

She was now wishing that she'd turned the lamps off, because she felt suddenly exposed with them on. Perhaps in the dark she wouldn't be so obvious. She hoped against hope that Anton's bolt was strong enough, because if not the consequences didn't bear thinking about. She was filled with a feeling of doom as she waited for the next move but not quite sure of what to expect.

But as her thoughts began to unravel in her mind once more, she tried to come to terms with what was happening: *Could it be that old woman – the voice was frail enough? Could she have been hiding all the time somewhere inside the house and Anton hadn't seen her when he'd searched? Did he search the top floor thoroughly, and was it really just a number of empty rooms with some odds and ends lying around as he'd said? He'd told her it was uninhabitable, but maybe she'd never moved out and had continued to squat in the place. Maybe she occupied the top floor. Maybe she was the one who had moved the rocker in front of the warm range, perhaps to use whilst no-one was at home.* Her head was full of maybes and was spinning with the strain of her imagination running rampant, but nothing made sense.

The fear began to subside, as compassion pushed its way through. What if she'd hit on the truth? Could it be possible that someone else was living in their home without their knowledge? It made more sense than anything else she could imagine. What if some poor old woman had been squatting in the rooms on the top floor all the time? That would explain how she'd come to see her when she first peered through the glass in the door.

Perhaps she should go and check if the old woman was there. As one compassionate human being to another, surely she could make her a cup of tea if that's all she craved for. But if her thoughts were willing, her body certainly wasn't. It remained huddled in a ball at the bottom of the duvet in a terrified state of suspense.

But while all those thoughts chased each other around in her head, she suddenly realised that everything had gone quiet. The creaking floorboards had stopped and there was no longer an eerie voice at the door. She listened intently, and as minutes ticked away there was still no sound. She finally raised her head from the duvet and looked towards the door. Nothing seemed to be happening and she was beginning to wonder if she'd imagined it after all. She remained perfectly still whilst anticipating another onslaught of eerie sounds, but after a while she was convinced that no-one was there.

She climbed out of bed and headed apprehensively towards the door. She leaned against it to see if she could hear anything but couldn't. After taking a deep breath she gripped the door handle and slowly turned it while sliding the bolt. She hesitated before pulling the door open, her body shaking in dreaded anxiety.

Her entire body tensed as she stuck her head out and looked around the drab and dreary landing and down the staircase and to the hall below. There wasn't a sound or sign of anything or anyone. Tiptoeing onto the landing and being careful to avoid the creaky boards, she ventured slowly down the stairs one by one. Her fear had not abated, but she knew she would have to check it all out if she hoped to settle down again for the night. She walked hesitantly across the hall and into the sitting room, the blood pumping through her veins like a train on a runaway track. The first thing she saw was the cushion on the floor again. It was back where it was earlier that day. A cold shiver ran through her spine as she knew it had nothing to do with her imagination, or nightmares, and this time there was no justification for how it could have happened. She couldn't escape from the truth. Someone was playing a cat and mouse game with her, but was unwilling to come out in the open.

Fear clutched at her heart again as she had no idea what she was dealing with, but at the same time she felt angry too. What was it about the house, and what sinister force could be trying to drive her away and why? She felt completely isolated and lonely, and the sheer terror of being alone in Juniper was overwhelming. But there was one chilling fact she now knew for certain: the incidents would only occur when Anton wasn't there.

She picked the cushion up, marched into the scullery and dropped it on the rocker once more. There was still a soft glow in the range and the burning embers continued to give out some warmth which helped to create a more pleasant atmosphere. She returned to the sitting room and threw some logs on the fire and decided to make herself a brew.

She sat down in the sitting room with her drink and it seemed to help to ease her nervousness, as somehow she didn't feel quite so trapped downstairs as she did in her bedroom. The fire began to burn merrily and soon the room took on a cosy feel. And as she became more relaxed, Lucy began to question her own fears and dilemmas. She knew in her heart of hearts that most women, when on their own, imagine that once they go upstairs and turn out the lights, in no time at all intruders will be lurking somewhere within the walls. That was fact!

But as Anton had wisely pointed out, why on earth do women imagine they are on the verge of being murdered in their beds, or about to suffer some other gruesome encounter once they turn out the lights? And why do they believe it's all going to happen once they lock up and retire upstairs. It may not make sense to most men, but the sad truth was: most women become fearful and imaginative in the dark – if they are alone.

Lucy leapt to her own defence in answer to the nagging fears that still clung to her. Juniper House was a big, eerie, sinister building and it was in a remote hamlet. It was also very secluded, and there was no doubt that she had experienced some rather strange encounters from the very first time they'd clapped eyes on it. Most men would feel nervous if they were put in the same position, so regardless of what Anton thought, it wasn't just because she was a woman.

Soon the heat from the fire began to make her feel drowsy and after a while she fell asleep. She didn't wake up until early morning. At first she couldn't work out why she had slept in the chair, but the memory of the previous evening soon came flooding back and she felt a cold shiver at the thought. She was stiff because she'd slept in an uncomfortable position and the house had grown cold. The fire was still in, although scarcely throwing out any heat, so she raked it and threw some wood on to bring it back to life.

She couldn't help but think about the previous night's incidents with some apprehension, still doubtful as to whether it was real, yet suspicious about the possibility of the old woman hiding somewhere – perhaps on the top floor. But she didn't dare investigate because she couldn't stand attics. She refused to venture up there even with Anton, although she had to admit that attics were not as frightening as basements. If fleeing for her life and they were the only two options, she knew full well which she'd choose to hide in, in such a dire situation; without a doubt she'd flee to the attics. But right now she wouldn't be fleeing anywhere because hopefully her life wasn't in danger, and she had no intention of venturing up there to find out whether or not they had a squatter. And so if that old woman was hiding upstairs, she would have to stay there at least until Anton came home. So until then it would have to remain a mystery.

As she reflected on how to tell Anton about her suspicions, she realised that she wouldn't really relish the idea of broaching the subject with him. He would think she was a nutcase, if he didn't think it already with what had gone on previously. But she would have to tell him about last night's incidents, regardless of whether she was certain or not of their reality. If that old woman was a squatter in their house she needed help, and desperately, and so they couldn't ignore it. And the more she thought about it, the more it calmed her fears, because having someone else in the house, even as a squatter, was better than her being alone – even if the thought did give her the creeps.

10

A COUPLE OF DAYS PASSED without incident, by which time Lucy had finally come to the conclusion that she must have been allowing her mind to get over-imaginative. It all seemed too distant from reality as time moved on and it was easy to imagine none of it had ever happened. After all, she hadn't actually *seen* anything.

She'd never taken to Juniper House from that first time they'd accidentally come across it, accentuated more by the old woman in ragged clothes who had stared back at her suspiciously from the foot of the stairs. As she'd peered through the pane of glass that day, she was horrified to think that someone lived in such squalor and even worse that they had been trespassing on her land. Anton was convinced that she'd seen her own reflection through the grimy window, which had probably become distorted due to lack of clarity. But Lucy, whilst she accepted that possibility, had always had doubts. Anton didn't seem to understand that she hadn't just seen a face – proving his reflection theory – she had seen a figure wearing ragged clothes, so how could he explain that? He couldn't and nor did he want to. He had grown impatient with her insistence that it had really happened and she had enough sense to drop it when she did. His only thoughts were about buying the place and nothing would deter him.

However, it was also feasible that she'd allowed paranoia to take over from that first experience and she'd let it feed her imagination, so there was a strong likelihood of Anton being right – after all, he nearly always did end up being right about most things. He was so laid back about everything and never got wound up, and he certainly didn't have an over-imaginative mind like she did. She'd never seen him angry – frustrated at her sometimes maybe, but never angry. He was, in her terms, cool, calm and collected and always in control. As she dwelt on his good points, of which there were many, it reiterated why she'd fallen in love with him from the very beginning. He was very meticulous about everything he did, and he never started a job without finishing it and it had to be perfect before he would call it complete. It was no wonder that she had built up the utmost confidence and trust in everything he said and did, convincing herself that he knew everything. She knew she leaned heavily on him to make all the important decisions in life, and by doing that she risked becoming a weak and fragile personality in herself, but it worked between them and she wasn't looking for change. She felt comfortable with him around and he was her tower of strength. No wonder she missed him when he wasn't there.

But what if this time he was wrong and the face had been real? The same old doubts still nagged and nagged – and yet, there was no other sensible conclusion without reverting back to the notion that she was hiding in the attics. Surely Anton wouldn't find *that* so hard to believe! She didn't know what to believe herself, so what chance had Anton got?

She busied herself in the house when at home and also volunteered to do extra days at work, so when Anton got home at week-end everything would be clean and tidy, and the extra money would come in useful to add to what Anton earned whilst working away. She was feeling quite pleased with how she had managed on her own, and she was sure that Anton would also be relieved that all was well.

However, it was not to be. The day before he was due to arrive home for the week-end, he had contacted her to say he wouldn't be back after all because he had chosen to work right through in order that he could finish the following week. It meant that he might even have the job finished by the following Wednesday. Lucy was devastated and whilst it was both bad news and good news at the same time, she was feeling somewhat dejected and disappointed, although she knew it was the best decision in the long run. Luckily her job was not restricted to weekdays and so she could volunteer to work at the week-end in order to keep herself occupied, and it also meant more money for the household pot. But she was feeling very lonely. The hamlet of Judge Fields was extremely desolate in the winter. No doubt it was busier in the summer months, but it was unlikely to attract a great deal of visitors. After all, there was nothing of interest apart from the old church, which, she'd heard along the grapevine, could boast the wedding of a very famous author which took place there long ago. There was only one road out of Judge Fields and it didn't lead to anywhere except the main road. There were several little lanes here and there, but they only led to a few scattered farms and no further, so one could only turn round and go back again. Once inside Juniper she felt closed in and isolated. There was really nowhere to go and as Anton had gone to Somerset in the camper van, any outings would have to wait until he came back; but then he would be busying himself doing jobs in the house, and so life was beginning to get tedious. It wouldn't be so bad if the pub was open; everyone dreams of a village pub in which to socialise and be part of the community. But it was all a myth as far as she was concerned because a community in Judge Fields just didn't exist. Everyone hid behind their curtains, and they were rarely, if ever, seen. Getting out of the house, apart from work, seemed to be a thing of the past, and if it continued for much longer she really *did* think she'd go mad.

Lucy's thoughts focused on Juniper House and how it seemed to get under Anton's skin from that very first moment. It was *love at first sight* – an obsession that she somehow couldn't understand. After all, it was just a big house, nothing more and nothing less, and nothing special to add to its merit. Although no doubt it had been a palatial home to someone else in the past when life was different, but nothing remained of its history now, at least not that she could see. Yet, as Anton had said it had potential, potential to start the business she had often fantasised about. But Judge Fields wasn't quite what she'd had in mind. Her fantasy of the tourist industry was more akin to St Ives in Cornwall, or some other idyllic place in the West Country where the climate was much milder than what they were accustomed to in the harsher North. She'd ruled out the Lake District as that was far too expensive, and the weather could be somewhat as damp as a wet squid for a huge chunk of the year. But this dead-end place? Who on earth would come here? Anton was convinced it would attract walkers and hikers, potholers, and anyone interested in the outdoors; and he had stacks of ideas of how to take advantage of it with guide tours and other related passions of his – nearly all outdoor pursuits. His ideas were overflowing, as well as challenging, and she couldn't keep up with them. He drew plans and wrote down every minute detail of all the concepts and designs which were in his head, and planned the outdoor activities with vigour. But Lucy didn't fancy hikers, walkers, potholers and suchlike, tramping through her nice new home with their muddy boots and heavy equipment – that is if they ever did succeed in making it a nice new home; she had her doubts. And his plans didn't exactly include her, oh no, she was going to be cooking, washing up, cleaning, shopping and generally being a servant to the public. Somehow her role in all of this seemed somewhat dreary and she certainly couldn't raise any enthusiasm for it.

The more she dwelt on it all, the more she felt that *she* was becoming a secondary figure in his notions. First it was Anton, followed by the house, followed by his ideas, and then followed by Anton – and finally, somewhere down the line came Lucy. The balance and order of things had somehow become re-arranged and instead of being first, as she always had been when they lived in their cosy, loving, little flat, she had somewhat become last in the pecking order. And as she began to fantasize about their lives before Juniper and Judge Fields, she was jolted back to the cold, harsh reality of how life had become. Anton was changing, his obsession had moved from her to the house, and the more it drew him in, the more it pushed her out. He was becoming a stranger to her. What if the house had a presence? What if the incidents which she thought she had witnessed, and now wasn't so sure, were deliberate by some unseen sinister force? Did the house have a past that couldn't be exterminated for some bizarre reason? Could that kind of phenomena exist? And had it got good reason for possessing Anton without anyone suspecting? And why choose Anton? Could *she* be in the way of something – or someone? The landlord of the pub had told them both to leave the house alone, the old man seemed to warn them too. What was going on? Her head was aching with the turmoil because she really didn't know the answers. But what if the house was truly haunted? She didn't want to ponder on *that* scenario either as it was much too frightening to take on board, particularly as she was going to be alone in it for quite a bit longer. She was beginning to wish she'd never allowed her thoughts to venture that far, because now she had frightened the life out of herself and she was tempted to find somewhere else to stay until Anton got back. But the truth was – there wasn't anywhere. She was stuck there whether she wanted to be or not! And she was now wishing that Anton was coming home at the weekend as first planned, so that she could have gone back with him and stayed in the camper van. No matter how hard a prospect that was, and knowing she'd have to force Anton to agree against his wishes, it would have been better than risking the plight of being in a haunted house alone. She shuddered as the reality of the whole scenario began to truly sink in, and she suddenly realised that she had inadvertently instilled a fear inside her head that couldn't be retracted. She wanted to revert back to the scenario whereby the old lady was hiding upstairs – another real human being, not a supernatural one; but it was too late now because the alternative was floating in and out of her head and wouldn't let go.

By the time Saturday had arrived, she had convinced herself once more that the incidents had definitely all been in her mind. She was also beginning to feel rather foolish at her paranoia, seeing as how nothing sinister had taken place since – other than in her mind! Fortunately she hadn't mentioned any of it to Anton – thank God!

She was spending as little of her time in the house as possible, due to additional working hours, so by the time she got to bed of an evening she was too tired to worry about silly things like ghosts. *Ghosts, how ridiculous could that be? Everyone knows they don't exist – not really, it's all make-believe, just like Santa Claus and fairies!* So for the time being she was able to put it all behind her.

That night she went off to bed early because the weather was pretty bad. It had rained nonstop all day, and by night-time it was obvious that a storm was brewing. The skies were blacker than black, and the wind was working its way up to a record speed. She'd put the old hot water bottle in the bed, wrapped her nightie around it, switched on her lamps and all was cosy and warm in there. The bedroom had become her refuge and once she'd locked herself in it she felt quite relaxed. So consequently the rest of the house ceased to exist in her mind. She read a few pages of her book and then settled down with Anton's pillow, which was her soother whilst he was away. She was getting quite confident at being alone in Juniper and was becoming rather chuffed with herself. Tucked up in bed with the heat of the bottle and Anton's pillow to cling to, she was feeling quite secure.

As she lay there in the still of the room, she could hear the wind gaining momentum as it gradually built up and began to hammer at the walls of the house, rattling the windows in the process. The sound of the wind whistling through the building seemed to echo in the vast empty spaces of the hall and upstairs. The noise was quite eerie and sinister and Lucy felt the sudden impact of her loneliness. She tightened her grip on the pillow and snuggled further under the duvet, her feet warming to the feel of the bottle. She hoped she would fall asleep soon and that the storm would be over by the time she awoke.

When she heard the sound of the old creaky floorboards along the landing, it caused her no alarm initially as she blamed it on the wind. Old houses creaked and groaned in the night, especially when almost empty of furnishings and carpets, and the wind would no doubt exacerbate it. She was more concerned about the battering of the house, as she lay there hoping there would be no damage done whilst Anton was away. But gradually, above the storm, she thought she could hear a soft whimpering sound. She tried to quieten her breathing so that she could listen, and once again had to hold her breath altogether. She knew the sensible thing would be to cover her ears and not let her imagination wander, but she could feel the palpitations building up inside.

"Mummy, where are you mummy?"

It was the distant cry of a child, and she shot up in bed.

She couldn't tell if the crying was coming from outside or not. Could it be a lost child in the tiny hamlet of Judge Fields? And where could it possibly have come from? She wasn't aware of any neighbouring families with children and the thought filled her with alarm and concern. But there was one thing for sure, regardless of the storm and any concerns for her own wellbeing, she would not hesitate to go out and search if she knew for sure the cries were those of a lost child.

But as she listened and concentrated, she began to realise that the sounds were coming from the landing area – and they were drawing closer to her bedroom.

"Mummy, where are you mummy?" followed by a faint tap on the door.

Lucy lost her nerve for a moment, and she almost shrieked as the horror of the situation took her by surprise. But despite the trembling of her body and the fear inside, she was also overcome by a strong feeling of compassion as she heard the distressing sound travel along the landing and away from her door. Regardless of the daunting prospect of going out onto the landing to investigate, she was sufficiently moved to want to follow the voice.

She climbed out of bed, slid into her slippers, and donned her dressing gown. After lifting the torch which Anton had left in a drawer for her, she walked gingerly over to the door and unbolted it. Opening it cautiously she peered across the landing and down to the big hall below. The lamps were struggling to compete against the vast open spaces and were beginning to flicker, no doubt because the old electrical system was no match for the storm outside. She felt the sudden attack of butterflies in her stomach as she began to imagine the consequences of the electrics failing, but it was too terrifying a thought to contemplate.

The hammering of the wind against the house was deafening, and the intermittent onslaught of lightening lit up the dark and gloomy hallway casting sinister and eerie shadows. But the voice could be heard again above the noise of the storm.

"Mummy, where are you mummy?"

The frail sounds were cries of anguish and they were coming from behind her across the landing. She turned swiftly and saw the shadowy image of a young boy standing outside the sealed-up door. He was staring at her pitifully, but she wasn't afraid. Her earlier emotions had been replaced by a sadness which was now almost reducing her to tears. And though the image was almost ethereal, she judged him to be around six years old. She could also identify that he had fair to blonde hair and striking eyes. He looked well-to-do by his appearance, and his countenance had an air of superiority about it. His features appeared to be of a highly intelligent, sharp-witted being, although refined and cultured in his manner. His attire, though old-fashioned, was beautifully designed and gave the impression that he was well-bred and came from a good background. She had calculated a lot in those few split seconds and she was immediately drawn to him.

Her curiosity now aroused she walked towards him, lighting her way with the torch along the dark and shabby landing, but he immediately turned his eyes away from the flashlight as she moved closer. She instantly stopped a short distance from him, careful not to frighten him away.

"Who are you?" she whispered gently.

He shielded his eyes with his hand but made no response. Lucy began to edge her way towards him again, but to her astonishment he vanished through the sealed door. She tapped on it lightly, it sounded hollow but there was no sound coming from within. All had gone quiet, apart from the storm gaining momentum inside the building. And then her attention was quickly diverted by sounds of a different nature coming from the direction of the secondary staircase that led to the attics. It was a noise which was unfamiliar to her, a distant whirring sound which she couldn't place. She was overcome by an unexpected calm as she walked over to the door that would take her to the staircase which led to the attics. She pushed it open gently and was greeted by a blast of cold air and darkness. She steeled herself against the stale smell of decay which oozed into the atmosphere as she stepped over the threshold. She remained motionless as she surveyed the inner space with its dilapidated grey walls and flaking plaster, highlighted only by the dim light projected from her torch. Scrawling initials and faint messages were scratched into the fading chalk of the decaying walls, the initial M being the most prominent. It was like peering into an old prison cell where one desperate being was clutching to life by writing on the walls. But the absence of any light, apart from the torch beam, made it impossible to read more. A cold shiver momentarily penetrated the dreamlike state which had descended upon her and numbed her senses to fear, but it didn't shake off her calm mood. She glanced up at the time-worn, curved staircase with its crumbling steps and years of dust and debris, not knowing where it would take her. But she still mounted them, hesitantly and slowly one by one. The distant sounds drew her to them as if magnetising her along the way and she felt compelled to continue. The fading light being projected from her torch which she tried to focus on in order not to stumble on the way up, exacerbated the dreariness of the walls and made the approach ever more unnerving and even threatening. She could almost make out a name on one of the walls part way up and she stopped to take a closer look. She could just decipher the first three letters – *MAG* – but the rest were too scribbly to make out. Had someone once been imprisoned in this cell-like place? It was too disturbing to dwell on.

Somehow she made it to the top of the staircase as it curved its way to a long, wide landing, and at that point she hesitated so that she could take stock of her surroundings. The whole experience was like walking into a tomb – dark, ancient and foreboding. Yet she felt no fear.

She could see the reflection of a light in the distance which was flickering on and off in harmony with the whirring noises. They had become louder and more significant as they echoed from across the landing. She walked towards an open door where the sound and light were clearly coming from. She peered inside the room apprehensively. It was dark and was being sporadically lit up by an old-fashioned film projector. The images appearing on a large white screen were black and white and it was very much like watching a home movie from the fifties. There was no sound except from the projector itself. The film running along the screen was of a happy family scene, taken in the grounds of Juniper. Cracks and interference were evident in the film, as she watched it portray a young child of about six-years-old playing cricket with his mother, a relationship which was obvious to the onlooker by the striking resemblance they bore to each other. The child wore white shorts and top and he had striking eyes and fair hair. The woman had a dazzling smile and her hair, which was tied back in a neat and sophisticated style, flattered her elegant and beautiful features. She wore a simple, but graceful dress with lightly padded shoulders, and she darted nimbly about as she bowled to the boy. Lucy was mesmerised for a few moments by the beauty of the woman, before realising that the boy in the film was almost certainly the same one whose shadowy figure she had seen disappearing through the sealed door. The whole scenario was surreal.

As the film continued through different scenes, a young girl with a surly expression appeared in the picture. She was followed by a male figure, a tall, slim man with smooth black hair and a dark trim moustache. He was wearing a multi- striped blazer and light coloured slacks and was holding a cigar. He looked very dapper. The girl however, who looked to be about ten-years-old, did not bear a resemblance to any of the others. Her manner appeared dull and abrasive as she watched mother and son playing happily together, and it was hard to work out if she belonged to the same family. The man stood by casually with one hand in his trouser pocket, as he observed the two at play. Lucy couldn't help but think that whilst he looked charming, polished and refined, he looked very much a ladies-man which was obvious by his body language, and somehow in the film he also came across as a cad and a bounder – it was just the way he looked.

The pictures flashed on and off as the scenes changed, but Juniper House stood gracefully in the background of each one. A large black car discreetly parked on the driveway in the distance, gave the impression of a privileged lifestyle. The house was meticulous and free of any plant growth burdening the stonework, and the floral and pristine gardens stretched for quite a distance into the background of the picture. It was a happy family scene clearly filmed on a warm summer's day, except for one slight contradiction – the young girl with the surly expression. She came across as a misfit, someone who didn't belong – and maybe she didn't. But that was something Lucy couldn't possibly determine.

Now convinced that the boy in the film was the one she saw on the landing, there was only one conclusion to be made – she had witnessed the boy's ghost, of that there was no doubt in her mind. And whilst the ghost of a child did not frighten her, there were questions to be asked. Why did he appear to her? What had he been trying to tell her? His appearance on the landing and his disappearance through the door must be because he was trying to relay a message to her, surely? What could it be? How was she to know or understand? One thing was for certain though, when Anton returned she would ask him to open up that concealed door and investigate what was behind it.

As she looked around the room she could dimly see an abundance of long trailing cobwebs everywhere, and the walls were dark and black with age. The windows were hardly visible due to grime and she could see an old fireplace in a corner. One wall was covered in blackboards to half-height, and stubs of chalk were lying in the channels. Faint remnants of messages were still visible on the boards, which could easily have been lessons from another age. She shone her torch around and it was obvious that it had once been a nursery, or school room. A faded rocking horse stood to one side of the room, clearly suffering from age and deterioration. Cobwebs stretched from one item to another, and an ancient and decrepit nursing chair stood forlornly in a corner, occupied only by a ragged teddy bear with one eye missing and a torn ear. The dampness of the atmosphere had clearly left its mark over time. A variety of wooden toys were piled neatly into boxes and a train set was placed in readiness on a track. Miniature cars and toy soldiers were scattered about the floor along with a large fort, mostly all mildewed. A day bed placed against a wall was made up with bedding suitable for a child, and whilst it had deteriorated with age it seemed to have stood still in time.

The whole room appeared to have been abandoned, almost as if the inhabitants had been evacuated without warning and had never returned. Then something else caught her eye, and she walked across the room aided only by the torch and the intermittent flashing of the projector. On top of a cupboard stood what could only be described as a small shrine. An old framed photo in black and white was surrounded by candles. When she looked closely at the faded picture she saw it was a young boy, the same one as in the film. Deteriorating with age and covered with cobwebs, it was beginning to crumble. But to her horror she saw a message scrawled into the dust on the cupboard which read: *'Where are you Billy?'* And it was evident by the freshly disturbed dust that it had only recently been written. But who, or what, could be responsible?

Suddenly out of the blue, she heard the sound of the train running around the track. Recoiling in shock she looked around her as the fear returned without warning, and the trance abandoned her to the reality of where she was. The projector stopped and at the same time the torch went out, leaving her in total blackness. The courage which had clung to her and aided her for so long had now failed and she began to quake with terror. The reality of where she was, alone on that floor, grabbed her by the throat as if to strangle the life out of her and she shook in absolute terror as she began to panic. Unable to negotiate her surroundings in the dark, her fear out of control, she could hardly utter a sound. Her heartbeat raced like an unmanned speedboat running loose and which had no possible chance of stopping, a situation which could only lead to devastation and destruction. Her heart was in her mouth as she fought against her fears and tried to grope her way out of that abominable place. Her screams which followed penetrated the silence like a knife slicing the life out of another human being, as her face got entangled with a mass of cobwebs. She frenziedly tried to claw them off, her rapid breathing drawing them closer to her mouth as she inhaled. They felt almost alive as they clung to her face, her nose, her eyes, and even her throat, driving her into a crazed state of frenzy.

Then to her horror she felt a strong presence in the room. She opened her eyes as best she could, and even in the darkness she could make out the dim outline of the old woman in rags. She was standing a short distance from her and was taunting her mercilessly. The sinister and threatening atmosphere almost drove her out of her mind, and as she stood there feeling trapped and vulnerable she thought with total certainty that there was a strong possibility she might be about to meet her doom.

Filled with blinding panic, she knew she must get out of there if she valued her life and her sanity. She fiddled with the torch but it had well and truly died. Darkness surrounded her, but against all the odds she tried to fumble her way to the door, and in those few seconds she became aware of what blindness must be like. She began to cry as she was unable to navigate her way out of that terrifying place, her feet trying to pace the floor as her hands groped the walls. She was freaking out, and was becoming concerned that fear and dread may take over and she would lose control of her mind. Could this be what had happened to the previous occupants? She suspected it must have been. She had to find the courage and ability to escape from there and make it back to her room otherwise she would succumb to the menacing forces that still clearly inhabited Juniper.

Thankfully she could remember the general direction in which she had come, and all it needed was a calm mind and positive approach if she hoped to get out of there. She took a deep breath and summoned up all the courage she could in order to calm her nerves sufficiently to be able to move stealthily towards the entrance that her memory was guiding her to. She groped the walls in order to feel her way there, but she tripped over some obstacle which had been invisible to the eye, and her fear multiplied tenfold as she fell to the floor. There was one advantage however, she fell midway through the doorway that would lead her to the landing and staircase which would be her escape route. She scrambled along the landing on her hands and knees in her haste to escape the demons of the night. She knew she was heading in the right direction, but didn't dare risk losing time by trying to get to her feet. Somewhere behind her, in the distance, she could hear loud, mocking laughter, almost like a witch's cackle. She moved even faster, her knees grazing badly as she crawled along at speed across the floor until she reached the turn of the stairway. She almost wept with relief.

Dragging herself to her feet she shuffled her way round the curve of the stairs. She descended the steps gingerly one at a time, feeling her way with her feet and sliding her hands along the wall. She almost collapsed with relief when she reached the bottom of the stairs and escaped through the door. She fled along the landing to her room and slammed the door behind her as she ran inside. As she leaned against the door trying to catch her breath, her legs wobbled like jelly. She slid the bolt to ensure the door was locked firmly in place, and remained where she was until her rapid breathing subsided. But when the horrible cackling sound started again, Lucy's chest suddenly tightened and she felt a strong jab at her heart which seemed to be slowly squeezing the life out of her. She couldn't move as she held tightly onto the door handle as if it were her refuge and the only way to keep the demons out. She knew she was having a panic attack and there was nothing she could do to abate it.

She looked over to a large set of drawers in the far corner. She knew they would be heavy and she may not be strong enough to move them, but she was frantic and who could say what inner strength a human being could provoke in a moment of sheer terror and doom. She rushed over to them and tried to move them, but they weren't for budging. She took out a couple of the heavy drawers and laid them on the bed and continued the practice until she felt the piece of furniture move. She could only shove it bit by bit towards the door in order to barricade it and it drained her of what strength she had, but she finally succeeded. She put the heavy drawers back into their spaces and felt confident that no-one could get into the room. She leaned against them, still breathless with the strain, but at least she felt safer barricaded in.

She clung to the drawers as she took deep breaths to calm her nerves, but her body began to tremble and her legs were weak. All her strength and energy had been sapped. She listened breathlessly to the echoing sounds of laughter and mirth as they invaded the empty spaces of the house. The wind, as it battered the walls outside and howled through the crevices in unison, seemed deafening. Lucy was convinced she was going mad. She pressed her hands to her ears to try to blank out the sounds, but it was impossible. But when she saw the flickering of the two bedside lamps as if the electrics were about to fail, she was overcome by the fear of being thrown into darkness in her only place of refuge. She had nowhere else to go where she would feel safe. And as her fears began to spiral out of control at the thought, she turned to see the old woman standing near the window grinning at her menacingly.

"Leave me alone," Lucy screamed. "What do you want with me?"

Her voice was breaking up as the panic set in, and the old woman seemed to sense it as she laughed triumphantly. Lucy was distraught, there was no hope left as far as she could see. She was finished – and there was nowhere else to run to. If that old woman edged one inch towards her she knew she would die of shock and then it would all be over. But the old woman just vanished before her eyes like the extinguished flame of a candle.

Like grease-lightening Lucy headed for the bed and scrambled onto it, hoping she could burrow her way to the bottom of the duvet in an attempt to shut it all out. She was gripped by a fear that she had never known before and she wanted to scream until her voice was hoarse; such was the terror that had engulfed her. But she remained there still and quiet, not daring to move in case she prompted the old woman to appear again. An eerie stillness seemed to have pervaded the room and Lucy didn't know which was the lesser of two evils: to flee from the house, or to remain in the sanctuary of her bedroom. Neither option offered much solace. The spirits which inhabited the house would not let her go, of that she felt sure, so there was no easy answer – she was trapped and she knew it. They clearly wanted something from her, but she had no idea what it was. And as she struggled to come to terms with the reality of the situation she now found herself in, the doubts that she had toiled with over and over again made way for the truth – the house was haunted.

Fixed rigid in her position on the bed, she sat and stared at the point where the old woman had appeared. She half-expected her to come back and she no longer felt safe now that she had invaded her space. The suspense did not last above a few seconds as she heard a faint voice, almost like a whisper, outside the door: "Billy, where are you Billy?"

Lucy realised it wasn't over and she screeched in fear as she buried herself under the duvet in an attempt to shut out the horrible sounds.

"Are we having a cup of tea?" followed by a light tapping on the door and the turning of the handle.

Lucy held her breath under the duvet. She had scrambled to the bottom and was holding herself in a ball, hugging her knees to her chest in an attempt to shield herself as she feared the worst.

"Are we having a cup of tea?"

As Lucy remained where she was, perfectly still and her heart beating furiously, she heard a different sound. The voice had changed to one of distress, anguish, pain and sorrow. Sobbing had now replaced the earlier menacing voice and had become that of a tormented woman.

"Is Billy coming home?" it cried over and over again.

Lucy's terror was beginning to subside as her emotions pulled her towards the compelling voice of anguish outside her door. She felt a tear trickle down her cheek as she was overcome by an agonising sadness which she found unbearable, and one which she had never known before. It was as if she was inside the head and heart of another human being. But she knew that no matter what, she mustn't give way to the feelings; she mustn't weaken, because deep down inside she was convinced it was a deliberate ploy by the spirits to lure her to them. And the consequences of that didn't bear thinking about. She remained glued to the spot, not daring to move, until the sobs disappeared to give way to the howling wind.

All Lucy wished for in that moment was Anton. She needed him to put his arms around her and make her feel safe. She cried helplessly, her mind confused and her heart troubled. Why had he brought her to this place? What had gripped him so strongly that he was prepared to risk their happiness by purchasing Juniper? How could he leave her alone in such a big, old, rambling and frighteningly sinister house? Why did he not believe that she had seen the old woman in the first place? He could have asked at the pub, and he could have investigated before being so keen to buy at any cost. Surely everyone must have known about it, that's probably why no-one had ever shown any interest in buying it. Would their life together ever be the same again? She wanted life to go back to the way it was in the flat, the happiness they shared, the fun and the loving. Now they had nothing, nothing but the monstrosity she had been left behind in. She felt like the sacrificial lamb which had been led to the slaughter. She felt demoralised, abandoned, frightened, and devastated at the situation she had been put in at no fault of her own.

Their lives had changed beyond recognition. There was no fun anymore because they were always too tired, and too short of money to be able to live any kind of life. It was all work. Juniper had robbed them of everything they had ever known and she couldn't understand why. Her fear also was that they were drifting apart. She felt unloved, uncared for, and insecure – emotions which she'd never had to deal with before. And the overriding fear was driving her into the ground. *Please come home, Anton, please,* she sobbed, her voice trembling uncontrollably. She no longer cared if her sounds could be heard, she let the tears flow relentlessly until finally the tiredness took over and she fell asleep.

During her troubled sleep, she dreamt that she was a young child being cradled by a beautiful woman with a rapturous smile who was gently humming a lullaby to her. It was a peaceful and heavenly moment and happiness filled the air, but after only a few seconds the woman's face changed to that of the old woman; she was menacing and there was a sense of madness in her features. Lucy awoke with a jolt, the fear pumping through her veins once more. The memory of the earlier incidents came flooding back, as she heard the sound of sweet music coming from the distance. It was the same melody as the lullaby in the dream, and she realised the dream must have been brought on by the music reaching her subconscious as she slept. She listened intently as the tune soothed her fears. It was haunting and soulful, but at the same time beautiful. It drugged her senses and she didn't want it to end. She had no idea where it was coming from and she didn't care, she just didn't want it to stop and soon she drifted into a deep sleep once more.

11

ANTON WAS DUE HOME at any time soon and Lucy was ecstatic. She had been badly affected by the dreadful incidents which she had experienced recently, and it had been on her mind a lot ever since. However, there had been no further occurrences and she was immensely relieved, particularly as Anton would be home at some point that day and therefore her nights of being alone were over.

She was feeling on top form as she got organised for work. She was only doing a part-time morning shift, as she wanted to finish early and get some shopping in and have the house nice and tidy for when he returned. She sat at the dining table with her mug of tea and toast and thought about how to tell Anton what had happened, and it wasn't going to be easy – but tell him she must.

Lucy knew full well that he wouldn't believe any of it had really happened, he would think it was her usual scatterbrain mind getting carried away with itself all because she had been on her own. But she needed to tell him so she could clear her head of the turmoil; she needed to share it and she needed him to understand. But most of all she needed him to comfort her and reassure her that she was still the most important person in his life and wouldn't allow Juniper House, or its demons, to come between them. And the only way to do that was to get rid of it – put it back on the market for sale.

But the doubts flooded her mind again. Would he agree to abandon Juniper? Would he truly believe the incidents did occur and weren't a figment of her imagination? Would the encounters happen again, but only when she was alone? Is that how it intended to tear them apart?

But even if he refused to believe her, but promised never to leave her on her own ever again, it still wouldn't be enough. She would be filled with doubts as to his genuine concern for her. Something in their relationship would die – trust! And how could they continue to live in a house whose previous occupants refused to let go?

Their relationship was going to be tested to the full. Everything hinged on his reaction once she relayed the events to him. If he doubted her and refused to take action – action of any kind which would reassure her of his devotion, she would be faced with a worse dilemma, she would have to leave him. And that thought filled her with dread and anxiety.

Her troubled thoughts moved back to the young child who she had witnessed outside the sealed door. She was still convinced that he was trying to relay a message to her. If Anton did agree to open it up, and she would have to make sure he did, perhaps something behind that door would explain the reasons behind the sightings. But what if there was nothing? Once again the niggling doubts pulled at her heartstrings and made her feel uneasy.

She got up and took her dishes to be washed, but as she approached the scullery she jumped back in shock and almost dropped them to the floor. The old woman was sitting in the rocker grinning at her jubilantly. Lucy couldn't take it in as surely she must be seeing things. But her legs threatened to buckle beneath her, and she felt numbed as the fear riddled her body once more. And before she could get a grip on herself, the woman had vanished into thin air.

Was this sighting a message, one which reiterated that the old woman, whoever she was, or had been, would triumph? Lucy was convinced that it was. The expression on her face and that grin and those eyes had said it all, and had left Lucy with no doubt in her mind. What she had just experienced reaffirmed in her mind that she was truly seeing another ghost. She had no idea who it was meant to be. Was it somehow connected to the images on the screen that she had watched that night on the top floor? The young boy who had appeared in the film, and also on the landing, could he be connected in some bizarre way to the old woman? She had no answers and no speculative thoughts about any of it. It was all too much of a mystery and they had known very little of the previous owners when they had purchased the house, so she had nothing to go on.

Her hands trembled as she continued over to the sink with her washing up. She did not hesitate to do what she had thought of doing in the first place, and that was to get rid of that old rocker regardless of what Anton might say. She was convinced that if she got rid of that, she would get rid of the old woman as well. Maybe, just maybe, she couldn't survive in whatever form she had adopted, without that rocker. It was a grim thought, but a possibility no matter how remote. She marched towards it and grabbed it with two hands and walked determinedly across the hall, out of the front door, and over to the skip where she dumped it unceremoniously inside. She moved swiftly back into the house and picked up the cushion and the blanket and did exactly the same with those. Slamming the front door behind her, she rubbed her hands together in satisfaction, convinced that *that* was the end of that!

She felt much better for what she'd done, she'd had it in mind for long enough but Anton's nostalgia had stopped her from carrying out her intentions. He wouldn't like it, but when it came to that old rocker she was past caring. Now the challenge was between her, Anton, and IT, because as far as she was concerned that old woman could now sit in that old rocker whenever she wanted to and haunt the skip instead of her. And she could travel with the skip whenever, and wherever it moved to while exploring new horizons. Maybe when it reached the tip, the rocker would be disposed of and then the old woman might disappear into the ether – but then maybe it was all just wishful thinking on Lucy's part as well. But right now she simply didn't care, because all that mattered was that it wouldn't be there when she got home from work.

Having tidied up and checked the time, she grabbed her coat and bag and left the house behind in order to catch the bus to work. Her excitement was increasing by the hour, as she looked forward to seeing Anton very soon.

Lucy arrived back home shortly after lunchtime feeling exhilarated. It had been the first time that they had both been apart and she hadn't liked it at all. Thank goodness it was only this once and soon he would be home for good. She hurried to hang up her coat, keen to unpack her shopping and prepare an evening meal for when he walked through the door. She couldn't wait.

She walked into the sitting room and as she approached the scullery she saw that the old rocker was back in its place. She was stupefied at first, but then realised that Anton must be back, and for a moment she felt guilty about him finding the rocker in the skip – maybe she had been a little hasty. She popped outside again, certain that his camper van had not been parked anywhere in the grounds when she'd arrived. It wasn't, so she presumed he must have nipped back out somewhere. Maybe he'd gone to the shops, perhaps to buy her some red roses to prove how much he'd missed her – but then as he didn't normally do that kind of thing it was probably most unlikely. But she enjoyed her moment of fantasy, although in truth just seeing him was enough.

She wandered back into the house and let her guilty feelings about the rocker penetrate her conscience. The fact that he'd brought it back in said it all. Now he was going to be annoyed at her. But she wasn't going to let it dampen their reunion – the old woman would like that wouldn't she? She must have felt really exultant when Anton challenged Lucy's behaviour by returning it back to where, in his opinion, it belonged – and with the rocker no doubt she came back too. She was no doubt gloating because she was in possession of the winning hand; but Lucy still had her cards to play – and who knows who would be the ultimate winner? Nevertheless a warm feeling of happiness spread through her veins knowing he was back and not very far away. Anton had been the best thing that had ever happened to her, and she couldn't wait to see his smiling face again.

She busied herself in the house, set the fire for when he returned, and everything was taking on a homely feel. The she heard a cat mewing. She was puzzled because it sounded as if the sound was coming from inside the house. She wandered through the rooms listening for where it was coming from. Anton must have let it in accidentally when he got back, and unwittingly trapped it inside. She could tell it was within close proximity by the sound of it. She stood still and concentrated hard as she listened, finally working out where it was coming from. There was a cupboard under the staircase which they hadn't yet got round to clearing out. It was just full of odds and ends which had been left behind, but that was where she determined the mewing was coming from. She opened the door and looked inside, but the noise had stopped. After a few moments she heard the sound again, but only faintly this time and it seemed to be coming from underneath a load of rubbish and cardboard boxes. She rummaged around to see if she could find anything, unconvinced that a cat could possibly have got trapped in there. But there was no denying it, she definitely could hear it.

At the bottom of the pile of junk, she could see a small, oblong, wooden box with metal hinges, but by now the noise had disappeared. Her curiosity aroused, she lifted the box and made a feeble attempt to brush off the years of dust which had accumulated on the lid. She placed it on the hall floor, knelt down beside it and opened the lid to look inside. There was an old piece of carpet which looked to be wrapped around something, so she lifted it carefully from the box and put it on the floor. It smelt stale and musty. She carefully undid the wrapping but jumped back in horror at what she saw. It was the skeleton of an animal which looked suspiciously like that of a cat. She quickly covered it up again and left it where it was for when Anton came back. It had freaked her out, because she couldn't come to terms with the fact that the mewing sound she'd heard seemed to have come from it. Obviously she must have been mistaken. Juniper was a big house and virtually empty of contents, so it would be difficult to ascertain where any sound was coming from. But although she tried to assure herself that that was the only answer, the fact it couldn't be heard anymore surely must speak for itself. A cold shiver ran down her back.

As the clock showed one hour after another passing by, Lucy was beginning to feel restless. She couldn't understand where Anton had got to, if, as she'd thought earlier, he had returned and gone back out again. And as the time reached five o'clock, she began to feel uneasy. What if he hadn't returned after all? That would mean that he wasn't guilty of having put the old rocker back in its place. Then who did? She suspected she knew the answer, but she didn't want to go there.

As darkness began to cast its spell once more, Lucy became jittery. She avoided going anywhere near the scullery, so that she wouldn't see that wretched old woman again. She now had no idea what time to expect Anton. She had been so delighted to think he had returned early in the afternoon, rather than late at night, that the true implications of that old rocker had not really registered in her mind. She knew now, if she hadn't known before, that she had a real fight on her hands and the old woman clearly didn't intend to give up – and that thought frightened the life out of her. She desperately waited for Anton as she paced the floor and avoided the hall where the old box was.

When he walked through the door at seven o'clock, she ran towards him and flung her arms around him, almost sobbing in relief.

"Whoa, steady on Luce," he exclaimed, as he put his bag on the floor. He picked her up, spun her around and gave her a big kiss. "Am *I* glad to be home," he said enthusiastically, walking her towards the sitting room with his arm wrapped firmly around her shoulders.

If Lucy had suffered doubts earlier, they were replaced with a strong conviction that he was just the same old Anton with just the same feelings about her. She was pleased, relieved and ecstatic.

But as they passed the hall Anton stopped dead in his tracks, his nose twitching.

"Can you smell something?"

She looked over to the parcel on the floor and hesitated. She hadn't really wanted to discuss that just yet, and she certainly didn't want to spoil their precious moment together.

"Oh, it's just some old rubbish I pulled out of the cupboard under the stairs. I was hoping to get it cleared out before you got back so it would be one less job to do," she fibbed.

"Well, I'll have to get rid of it whatever it is, it stinks!"

They wandered arm in arm to the sitting room and Anton's face lit up at the sight of the roaring fire. He slipped his arm off her shoulder and walked directly to the scullery.

"I see you moved the old rocker back?"

"No – I thought ..." but then she hesitated as she realised the implications of what she was about to say. This was not the right moment. "Err, sorry, I mean yes, I'd forgotten to be honest. I thought it would stay warmer in there for you," she fibbed again.

She had never lied to him before and she didn't want to start now. They had always had a very open and honest relationship – at least before Juniper that is. Now she'd been made to break that bond between them and that saddened her.

"Oh that's really thoughtful of you Luce." He gave her a hug and a peck on the forehead.

Now she *really* felt guilty.

"Tell you what Luce that smell coming from the range beats that stink in the hall. While you're rustling up that grub – let me guess, it's a stew – I will dump that rubbish." His face beamed at the thought of his favourite dish and he disappeared before she could answer, so she left him to it while she sorted out their tea.

Anton looked curiously at the item on the hall floor and couldn't resist opening it to look inside. He could see it was the remains of a dead cat and he wrinkled his nose. Carefully covering it again, he put it back in the box and pushed it under the stairs before joining Lucy in the sitting room.

"No wonder it smelt Luce, it's a dead animal. I've wrapped it up again and put it back in the box, which will act as a coffin. I'll bury it later in the grounds. It must have been someone's pet and for one reason or another they didn't want to part with it. Sad when you think about it. But I'll give it a good burial I'm sure whoever owned it would be happy for me to do that." He washed his hands in the old sink and sat down at the table.

Lucy had hoped he would dump the carcass in the skip, as she didn't want it staying around for longer than necessary. She was convinced that the mewing sound must have come from it, no matter how outrageous that would sound when she told him. The trouble was, the longer she put off telling him the harder it was going to be. She began to feel dejected again as she realised the difficulties ahead of her and the decisions she may have to make if he didn't believe her. She put two bowls of stew on the table and sat down beside him feeling quite disheartened.

"That smells delicious Luce. It's my favourite." He got stuck in as if he hadn't eaten for a week.

After a few minutes Anton noticed that Lucy was looking very down at the mouth.

"Don't let it upset you Luce, that dead animal will have belonged to someone who probably died years ago. There could be umpteen reasons why they left it in the box. It was probably forgotten. I didn't mean to make you feel sad, I just speak first and think afterwards – bad fault of mine. But I'll soon have it sorted." He squeezed her arm reassuringly.

But Lucy didn't care who the dead animal belonged to, she just wanted it out of the house. The thought of it being under the stairs in that cupboard was freaking her out. What if she heard it again – but then she suddenly realised that if it started its mewing now Anton was home, surely he would hear it and then she could tell him all about the house being haunted without the fear of him not believing her. At least she could hope.

After eating, Anton lifted the old rocker from the scullery and put it in front of the fire in the sitting room. He sat down and exhaled a yawn of contentment as he stroked his stomach in satisfaction.

"I can't tell you just how much I wanted to get back to this house of ours. That's why I volunteered to work week-ends so that I would get home sooner, which means I can get started on the jobs more quickly. I knew I was missing it, but sitting here makes me realise now exactly how much." He sat back and sighed. Within minutes he had closed his eyes and was snoring.

Lucy looked at him for a few moments, he was so content. Normally she would have loved him even more for it, but somehow she felt troubled. He hadn't mentioned missing *her*. On the contrary, his thoughts had been all on the house since he returned. In fact the more she dwelt on it, the more she realised that he hadn't told her he'd missed her at all. The doubts were welling up inside her once more, and the tender thoughts she'd felt earlier were beginning to disintegrate. And what's more she was beginning to worry. If things didn't improve between them, if he continued to put the house before their happiness, the consequences would be unbearable. It would divide them permanently and she wanted to avoid that at all costs.

She tidied up and washed the dishes whilst Anton still slept. She could understand him being tired, after all he'd had a long drive and he'd been working non-stop without a break. But she was left with little or nothing to do except more housework, and she was feeling frustrated that they weren't spending precious time together, after being apart for so long. It was understandable, but dreadfully disappointing for her. And so she browsed nonchalantly through some of the old books which had been left behind in the bookcase, but they were mostly educational and completely lost on her. They were also damp and musty and eventually they would have to be discarded when they got round to it.

After a while she unpacked Anton's luggage and put his clothes in the wash, but after running out of things to do, as well as energy, she decided to waken him. He awoke with a grunt, but was finally persuaded to go to bed. Lucy had put the hot water bottle in bed so that it would be warm and snug for him, but he didn't even seem to notice as he was fast asleep as soon as his head touched the pillow. He didn't even kiss her goodnight. His back was turned to her, so she snuggled up to him and put her arms around his waist, just content that he was back and they were together.

In the early hours of the morning Lucy was awakened suddenly by the sound of a cat mewing. At first it was distant then it seemed to move closer to the bedroom. She thought perhaps she was still sleeping and the mewing was part of the dream, until she heard the floorboards creaking and she shot up in bed. She woke Anton up abruptly by shoving him rigorously, which he wasn't much pleased about.

"Anton, listen, that cat's outside the bedroom door, I've just heard it." She was actually whispering.

He turned his head slightly and looked at her, his eyes hardly open, and after gawping for a few moments he turned over and went back to sleep.

"Anton," she whispered, giving him a hard nudge in the back. "Listen, it's at it again, can't you hear it?"

He turned his head and looked at her again, but this time a look of disdain spread across his features and for a moment he thought he was dreaming. As he was about to nod off again, Lucy grabbed his arm and shook it vigorously to bring him to his senses. He jumped up, his face like thunder.

"There is no cat," he yelled. "Go back to sleep and stop being stupid. You've obviously been dreaming." He pulled his arm from her grasp and turned over once more, by which time the mewing had stopped.

By this time Lucy was wide-awake, so she jumped out of bed and decided to look for herself. She opened the bedroom door, looked out onto the landing and down into the hall below, but there was no sign of anything. She began to question her own sanity, and even worse she didn't relish Anton's reaction the next morning – if he remembered the incident at all.

But as delayed reaction set in, she found herself pondering on Anton's expression when she'd shook his arm. She'd never seen him like that before. In fact, she could hardly take it in. He was furious with her, it was written all over his face. He looked strange, almost as if he was about to strangle her, or something like that. But she couldn't help it, she thought defensively. She'd definitely heard the cat mewing and the floorboards creaking, so what did he expect her to do, roll over and go back to sleep as if it had never happened?

Her thoughts were in turmoil again and threatening to spiral out of control. Maybe it hadn't happened. Maybe she was going crazy after all. Maybe, just maybe, this house was driving her insane, just like its previous occupants. Maybe *she* will one day roam the house and make the floorboards creak, and scare the living daylights out of somebody – when *she* too, perhaps, has become a ghost – just like vampires turn *their* victims into more vampires. But now she was becoming irrational, as well as delusional, as well as neurotic and hallucinatory and ... for a moment she hesitated in her thoughts as the memory of Anton's words slowly seeped into her mind. He'd called her *stupid* and she'd only just realised. The Anton she knew would never have done that. Something strange had come over him and she didn't know what. All she knew was that they had to get out of this house and leave it forever. She would be insane not to demand it, and Anton would have to face up to the truth. It was haunted, whether he wanted to believe it or not, and as neither of them had ever had any experience of ghosts, or suchlike, how could they know what their intentions were, or what they would stoop to? Their lives could even be in danger! She'd never thought of that before, because she'd been so hell-bent on believing that the house and its demons were only intent on driving her mad. But what if that was what she was meant to believe, while they steered her in the wrong direction and away from the truth, whatever that truth may be. She had stimulated her brain so much that she couldn't possibly go back to sleep. She couldn't get the thoughts out of her head and she was becoming confused and muddled, and her brain felt like scrambled eggs. She pulled on her dressing gown and slippers and went downstairs, her fear having seemingly subsided.

She saw that the fire in the sitting room was still lit, so she gave it a stir and decided to boil some water to make a brew. She glared at the rocker as she walked past it on her way to the scullery, and for a joyful moment she imagined herself chopping it up for firewood and using it on the fire. Oh how she wished!

She sat down in front of the fire with her brew and warmed her hands on the hot mug. She felt quite angry at Anton's reaction, even after taking into account that he would be shattered from his journey home. She appreciated that she'd wakened him suddenly from a deep sleep, from which he would normally be hard to resurrect at the best of times, but what if they'd had a burglar? Would he have said the same things to her then, just because he'd been wakened from his slumber? And more importantly, would she ever feel safe again knowing that he wouldn't react in a responsible manner if for any reason she had to wake him up suddenly? And as her thoughts began to travel again at great speed, they were rudely interrupted by the sound of a cat mewing.

She put her drink down quietly on the fireplace and slowly tiptoed towards the hall from where the sound was coming. She stopped dead in her tracks at what she saw next. The faint outline of a ginger and white cat was strolling nonchalantly across the hall, before disappearing through the cupboard door – which was closed – under the stairs. It was a spine-chilling experience and the hairs on the back of her neck stood up. She wasn't afraid of a cat, dead or alive, but seeing it going back through the cupboard door and no doubt into its box freaked her out. It all seemed so surreal. Did the cat belong to that old woman, she speculated? Was the old woman a witch? She'd often suspected it – and a dead cat as her accomplice did rather fit the bill.

But it was all constantly preying on her mind, and the worry of it was making her feel overstressed. She didn't want to share it alone and why should she? It was never her idea to buy Juniper. The house oozed creepiness and bad vibes, and she could sense it strongly. She hurried back upstairs and jumped into bed. Anton was by now dead to the world and snoring, clearly unaware of what was happening whilst he slept. She pulled herself close to him, wrapped both arms around his waist and snuggled into his warm body. She felt him stiffen in his sleep as his warm body reacted to her cold one. Right now she didn't care about the things he'd said, or what he might think of her the next day, she just needed to know he was there and she wasn't alone.

12

THE WEEK-END seemed to come quickly, much to Lucy's relief. Anton was supposed to have had a few days off when he returned from being away during the week, but he'd decided to go to work instead. Lucy was puzzled, because she'd taken the time off her own little job so they could spend a few days together to make up for the long absence, so she was feeling pretty miffed that she'd spent the remaining week alone again. He had been very subdued ever since the 'cat' saga and she was not too happy about that either. She still felt that she was in the right and that he was being unreasonable – especially if he had got the sulks because of it. After all, she was the one who'd been most disturbed. What did he know about it anyway – he'd just slept through it and left her to it! From then on he'd hardly spoken to her at all, he just grunted whenever she tried to talk to him, and when they were in bed he turned his back on her. Lucy was feeling dejected again. If anyone had ever told her that they would have a minor tiff which would lead to such an emotional and upsetting rift between them, she wouldn't have believed it. Up to now they had always been inseparable. Would this have happened if he'd never gone away? She had no idea, but one thing she did know: it wouldn't have happened if they'd never clapped eyes on Juniper House.

She still hadn't managed to psyche herself up to give him the bad news about the house being haunted. And as time was moving on, it was becoming even harder still. She really wanted him to open up that sealed door, because she had a strong feeling that it held the clue to what was going on. She knew that it wasn't one of his priorities, and he was leaving it until the more important jobs were done. But it was important to Lucy – if only she could get round to telling him.

Lucy woke up the next morning and rubbed her eyes. She turned to snuggle up to Anton but soon realised he wasn't there. She sat up in bed abruptly. She glanced at her bedside radio and saw the time was eight o'clock. It was Saturday morning and Anton must have been up at the crack of dawn, because his side of the bed was cold.

She got washed and dressed, tidied up the bedroom and went downstairs to be greeted by the appetising smell of bacon wafting through the air. Anton had lit the fire and the range, and everything was looking clean, tidy and welcoming. The old rocker was in front of the sitting room fire, the table was set for breakfast and Lucy was relieved that he was back to normal – at least she thought he was.

She walked up to him and greeted him with a hug but he didn't respond.

"If you sit at the table, breakfast is ready, it won't be a minute," he said brusquely.

Lucy obeyed him like a child who had just been scolded for being naughty. She was mystified by this new Anton and had no idea what had come over him. And why was it that whenever Anton moved that old rocker anywhere, it didn't move itself back to its original position in front of the scullery range? *She* couldn't even walk past it without feeling threatened. She was convinced it was that old woman who was stealing Anton from her. *Yes, of course, that's it!* Her thoughts were spiralling out of control again. If that woman wants Anton so strongly, that she is prepared to drive Lucy away by putting the fear of god into her, then she will have a fight on her hands because Lucy did not intend to give in. She was still convinced that the child she saw disappearing through the sealed door was trying to communicate with her, and it was up to Lucy to toughen up and spur Anton into action. But it was easy to contemplate, but not so easy to do, so she decided to wait until they'd eaten breakfast before attempting to pluck up sufficient courage to face the music.

They ate in silence, although Lucy had made several attempts to converse, but he clearly was having none of it. Then she began to wonder if his mood was perhaps nothing to do with the cat saga at all. Maybe he'd had some problems whilst working away. She hadn't thought of that before, and she was beginning to feel guilty all at once. Maybe he was upset about something – maybe he'd lost his job. Oh god! That thought had never occurred to her. One thing was for certain, he was deep in thought and she needed to find out why.

"Is there something wrong Anton? Anything I need to know about?"

"No!" came his frosty reply.

She was a little taken aback, because at least she'd expected the courtesy of a more reasonable response.

"Well something's clearly wrong and I think I have a right to know what it is."

But he just got up from the table, cleared the dishes and proceeded to take them into the scullery.

Lucy jumped up and followed him. "Here, let me do the dishes."

Anton ignored her and continued to do them himself. It was so out of character that Lucy was beginning to get tetchy. She grabbed his arm and stopped him from carrying on.

"Are you going to tell me what's wrong or not? You've been like this ever since you arrived back – or at least ever since I heard that cat."

What she had just said evidently touched a raw nerve. He swung round and stared at her like a madman.

"Can't you get it into your silly head – there was no cat!" he bellowed, causing Lucy to jump back in alarm.

So that was it! The cat saga had turned him into a monster and it was one that she didn't much like. She wanted her old Anton back because somehow something, or someone, had possessed him, and she needed to act fast otherwise he was dangerously close to turning into one of the demons that was unmistakably inhabiting Juniper House.

"Well, whether you like it or not, this house is haunted!" she blurted.

Lucy was getting her mad up which was evident by her rebellious stance, and there was no stopping her.

"That cat isn't all I've heard, and what's more I've even seen it as it disappeared through that door under the stairs – and what's more the door was closed when it went through it."

She wagged her finger towards the sitting room.

"And what's more that stupid old rocker that you seem to have adopted is haunted as well."

She stamped her foot in retaliation and winced as it hit the hard stone floor.

He stared at her as if she'd grown two heads. But it didn't deter her. Her eyes flashed in defiance as she pelted him with all the experiences she'd witnessed over the past few weeks.

Having got up on her soap-box there was no holding her back.

"You'd better believe it Anton this house has other inhabitants besides us. And what's more they don't want me here. Or to be more precise: SHE doesn't want me here." She pointed her finger to the old rocker. "She wants YOU!"

Anton glowered at Lucy, his face clouding in anger as he turned on her.

"You never wanted to come here, did you? You had your mind set on staying where we were forever. You just wanted things to stay the same because you don't like change. All that talk about having a B & B was all it was – just talk. You never intended to *live* the dream it was just a fantasy to you and nothing else. Well we obviously don't think the same, do we? Because *I* do want to live the dream, I do want to better myself and I intend to do just that." His tone was sneering, his face twisting in rage.

Lucy was stupefied and stared after him as he stormed off. She heard the door slam, and minutes later she heard the van driving off. She couldn't take it in. Was this really happening? She flopped down in the nearest chair and tried to think.

As she began to simmer down the tears came. She adored Anton, she didn't want to lose him and she must get her head together. If she continued to antagonise him in a way that would compromise their relationship there would be no turning back, and the house and that old woman would win. She needed to think clearly. She had to have a master-plan if she wanted to keep Anton and fight off the demons. At least that row had forced her to confront the truth: that she could not lose Anton, as he was all she had and all she wanted. And deep down Lucy knew that it wasn't Anton's fault. He had been taken over by some strange and sinister force which belonged to the house and he was helpless against it, unless she could find a way to overturn it. And overturn it she must.

Common sense always prevails in the end, and as she analysed the situation she came to the conclusion that she needed to show more interest in the property, otherwise she was playing into the hands of the evil forces who were seeking to destroy their relationship. She needed to show more enthusiasm for their new home and share the challenges that they faced in achieving their final goal. She should encourage him more and show more gratitude – the list was endless; and she was also beginning to realise how unfair she'd been about it all. Anton had been over the moon when he first discovered Juniper on that eventful day in Judge Fields, which had begun with them both looking for a former site where gallows may have once been erected. That intriguing search caused them to stumble across the house hidden behind that chaotic garden. She felt a warm breath of happiness sweep through her as she recalled their happiness that day, until she'd spoilt it all by insisting that she'd seen an old woman peering at her from within the house. From that very moment she'd shown absolute disinterest, only wanting to continue their journey to their favourite destination. How selfish of her and how disappointed Anton must have felt. But through his persistence and sheer determination, they had ended up as property owners instead of renters. Why could she not have been more encouraging and more grateful? She was now seeing herself in her true colours, instead of constantly brooding about the dark side of Anton. No wonder he felt the way he did. He had directed his anger towards her because she'd let him down, and not because he didn't care as she had so vehemently convinced herself ever since they'd bought the house. He was right when he'd said she didn't like change. She didn't want to spoil their perfect little life. She wanted it to go on and on. Well now she knew the truth there was only one course of action. She had to make it up to him, and hopefully break the spell that the spirits had cast on her unsuspecting Anton.

But that didn't sort out Lucy's dilemma regarding the ghosts, because she knew they existed and she knew she was never going to convince him. However, she would worry about that later. First of all she had to regain control of their love for each other, and remove the sinister hold which had been put on Anton. One thing for certain they couldn't all live under the same roof together.

But maybe it was simpler than she thought. Perhaps if she changed her attitude towards the house – and that rocking chair – maybe the ghosts would disappear, and that would solve her problem of having to tell Anton after all. Maybe they were antagonised by her negativity towards Juniper, and maybe their intention had simply been a warning call to wake her up to the fact that if she continued in her crusade against Juniper she would lose Anton. *Yes, that's the reason behind it all,* she thought. So they were friendly ghosts really, if she gave them half a chance, and to do that she must learn not to fear them.

She had covered every scenario possible during her time at Juniper – and right now she was convinced she'd just hit on the *real* truth once more, and therefore she could safely reject all of her earlier suspicions.

She felt elated and relieved, as if an enormous weight had been removed from her tiny shoulders.

She jumped up from the chair and considered how best to put her plans in motion. She would make Anton his favourite stew again. She still had time to catch a bus to the shops and get what she needed. She was determined to let him see she was still the same person that she'd always been, the one he'd fallen in love with at first sight. And she knew how to make him happy. That big black cloud which had followed her around since moving to Judge Fields had now gone, and she was feeling much happier.

Later that day when Lucy returned from the shops, she noticed the van in the drive so she knew Anton was back. She felt happy and relieved, and there was a spring in her step as she opened the front door. Somewhere in the distance she could hear him hammering and banging and so she disappeared into their make-shift kitchen to prepare the tea. She weighed up how content she ought to be as Anton worked away in the house and she prepared dinner. This was the bliss that all loving relationships were made of – what more could she want and how could she have been so blind? Working together on their new home, and knowing they owned it, was the stuff every young couple dreams of, and from now on she would be a changed person with a totally different view about Juniper.

She laid the table with a pretty tablecloth which she had treated herself to whilst out shopping and placed a candle in the middle of it. It was simple and cheap but it gave the right ambience. She had treated them both to a bottle of wine, as part of her plan to create an intimate and romantic setting. It was a delayed celebration to welcome him home, and she hoped that Anton would be pleased at her efforts.

By the time she was ready to serve dinner, Anton had finished what he was doing and had gone for a shower. When he came back down the table was set, the candle was lit and the wine was served. He walked into the room and evidently couldn't wipe the smile from his face. She knew her plan was working.

"Sit down Anton I'm sure you've worked up an appetite." She pulled a chair out for him before disappearing into the scullery. She returned with two dishes of stew which she placed on the table. Before sitting down she put her arms around his neck and whispered sultrily in his ear: "I'm sorry for making you mad and for being so unreasonable and silly. I'll make it up to you later."

There was a distinct improvement in Anton's mood, and the cloud of thunder which had spread across his features earlier had disappeared. Lucy was thrilled.

They tucked into their meal, and after clearing the dishes away they sat in front of the fire. Anton relaxed in his rocker as they both finished the bottle of wine. The heat of the fire was making them feel drowsy after a hot meal and alcohol, and when Lucy saw his eyes drooping, she suggested they go to bed early and spend some time together. Anton knew exactly what she meant and he woke up in an instant at her recommendation. They mounted the stairs arm in arm, and everything felt as it should be. It was like starting all over again.

As they settled down to enjoy a romantic moment together, Lucy took the lead in an effort to make him feel good, and he responded with a passionate kiss as he settled into some serious love-making. But at that crucial moment, Lucy thought she could hear music playing from somewhere downstairs. A soft melancholy tune resonated throughout the house, and there was no mistaking that it was real. It sounded like someone was playing a violin.

Lucy pulled away from him and said: "Listen, can you hear that?"

Anton tried to pull her back towards him again, but she was too distracted.

"Listen, can't you hear it?"

"Hear what?" he said in a sensual voice, his only concern being to stimulate her passions.

"That music," she hissed, pulling away from him altogether to sit up.

Anton didn't seem to know what was happening. One minute he was enjoying a seductive moment – or two, and the next he was sitting alone on the bed. He was perplexed as he'd stared blankly ahead and watched Lucy's naked body disappear out of the door. She had scrambled out of bed and was listening from the landing.

"Anton, come on, you'll be able to hear it from here," she called to him in a low voice.

He crawled off the bed and reluctantly joined her on the landing. He couldn't hear a thing. In fact everything seemed peaceful and quiet, and he wondered why they were both shivering out there in the cold.

"Come on Luce," he pleaded seductively as he nibbled her ear. "I can make much better music than someone outside passing in their car."

But she pushed him away. "Listen," she insisted. "You must be able to hear that. And it's not outside, it's in the house!"

"I can't hear anything," he said, as he pulled himself together with a jolt. "All I can hear is you rabbiting on about something and nothing. What does it matter if someone's playing music outside anyway? Maybe someone's having a party – so what!"

"A party – in Judge Fields, this dead hole, you must be joking! They wouldn't know a party here if it hit them in the face." She was at it again and had just ruined what she had begun, but she couldn't stop herself.

Anton looked at her in exasperation, his erotic notions having now gone completely out of his head and out of his system altogether. She had put a stop to that good and proper. He rushed into the bedroom, grabbed his dressing gown and bounded downstairs. He searched the hall and sitting room, and moved around the house slamming doors on his way. The music by now had stopped, so Lucy knew she was well and truly in deep trouble.

She followed sheepishly down the stairs, not sure if she could face him or not. He was right of course the music had probably been coming from someone's car, maybe someone visiting a neighbour. She'd really put her foot in it now, and she doubted her ability to resurrect any further urges from Anton of a passionate night together. She'd blown it and she knew it.

He marched back into the sitting room where Lucy was waiting with a guilty expression on her face. She had boiled the kettle in an attempt to pacify him with a brew. He didn't say a word, which only acted to make Lucy look, and feel, more embarrassed and shamefaced. She wished she could crawl under the table without him noticing. But he noticed.

"You've got a serious mental problem, do you know that?" he bellowed.

His stormy outburst came out of the blue and made her jump.

Lucy looked at him dumbstruck. There was no way she was standing for *that*.

"And you are just a male chauvinistic ..." she was struggling for words.

"Just listen to yourself babbling – you can't even finish a sentence can you? That's all you seem to do these days – babble, babble, babble. You're driving me insane! If I listen to you much longer I'll be following in the footsteps of whatever mad hatters lived here in the past."

He was fuming and she had never seen him quite like that before. She gawped at him, her mouth open and her thoughts racing. She was absolutely flabbergasted. Where did this guy come from? Had she met him before somewhere? Was he an imposter? And where was her lovely, docile Anton? She voiced her thoughts loud and clear.

"I don't know who you are anymore. You're not the person I met – far from it – you're just an imbecile, a madman who can't see what's right under your nose." She'd never yelled before and her voice was beginning to croak.

"I suggest you take a good look at yourself before you start throwing slurs at anyone else. Anyway, I've had enough of all this, you're just a complete nutter, you should be locked away."

Lucy marched right up to him, and tilted her chin so she could scream in his face.

"Now you listen to me. You're the most selfish, self-centred sod I've ever had the misfortune to meet. Whether you like it or not, this house is haunted. Just because you haven't seen anything, or heard anything, means absolutely nothing. You've been wearing blinkers ever since you first set eyes on this place. I HAVE seen what's occupying this place, and we've invaded their sanctuary and they don't like it!"

She suddenly realised she'd caused a crick in her neck through tilting her head back so far and screaming out loud. It was his fault of course; why did he have to be six foot and four inches tall when she was only five foot two? She had to massage the back of her neck before she could continue, which only acted to give him more time and space to jump back in whilst she was temporarily disarmed.

"Well you clearly don't like this house, so it might be a better idea if you go back to the flat. I'm sure there won't have been a queue of people waiting to take a poxy little 'pied-a-terre' – because that's all it was, a glorified bed-sit! Little places suit little people."

It was getting nasty.

"How dare you?" Lucy spat at him. "And you'd better remember that this house is part mine as well as yours and I could force a sale." He didn't like that and it rendered him speechless.

At that point they both clammed up. Neither of them knew quite what they were fighting over, or how it had all begun and why on earth it had got so out of control. Anton was suddenly scratching his head, and he seemed confused as if he'd just wakened up from a trance. He suddenly remembered that Lucy had interrupted a crucial moment in bed with her insane ramblings and he felt rightfully peeved; but he would never have normally reacted in such a manner. He felt ashamed and guilty and couldn't understand what was going on. Could he be wrong? Could she have seen or heard something? But he answered his own question: *No, she couldn't have, after all he would have seen or heard it too.* His head was being invaded by a sudden attack of numerous thoughts, as he toiled and laboured to work it all out.

He had suspected from the beginning that she wasn't going to settle in Juniper, She had made that clear from the outset by her body language and the little things she'd said. But he knew what was best, and had decided she would come round to it in the end. It was probably her imagination working overtime whilst he was away. He knew she'd be nervous at being alone, but they needed the money and therefore the chance to work away on a big job was an opportunity not to be missed. He hadn't told her that he'd volunteered of course, because she wouldn't have stood for that. He sighed deeply, flopped down in the old rocker, and stared at the burning embers in the grate; his heart was deeply troubled and his mind confused.

Lucy, meanwhile, had simmered down somewhat. She went into the scullery and made the brew that she'd started on earlier and brought in two mugs. She put one down on the fireplace for Anton and sat in the chair opposite with hers. She felt much better for having exhausted herself with her tantrum and maybe Anton did too. They had probably been spending too much time working on the house and not having time for anything else, because it was completely out of character for them both. They'd never had a row before, and the situation had clearly brought out the worst in them. She'd never behaved like that in her life. Could the house and its inhabitants be poisoning her mind against Anton, so much so that her unpredictable behaviour pattern would eventually cause the ruin of them both?

They remained silent as they drank their tea. Lucy felt shamefaced and concerned as she looked at Anton and saw the seriousness in his face. The untimely argument may have scarred their relationship for ever, and Lucy did not want to consider the consequences. She knew deep in her heart that the house was to blame. Anton had changed personality because of it, nothing would convince her otherwise. No matter how much she repeatedly justified his reactions by blaming her own behaviour, she always returned to the notion that someone, or something in the house was driving them apart. Granted, she may have made a mistake about the music she'd heard. She hadn't considered it coming from outside before, mainly because it was so dead in Judge Fields that if a pin dropped outside she'd be able to hear it. But nothing could alter the fact that the house was haunted.

"I've got an idea," Lucy said without flinching. "If you agree to remove that door upstairs which has been sealed up, and if there is nothing in there to throw a light on what I've seen or heard, I will agree that you're right and I'll make an appointment to see a psychiatrist." If she hoped to pacify him with that sudden display of submission she was wrong, and anyway he probably wasn't daft enough to believe her. He didn't answer he was just too deep in thought.

Lucy took the gamble and without warning threw the whole experience at him which she'd encountered.

"Well you're not likely to believe this, but I saw a small boy outside that sealed door and as I approached him he vanished through it." She didn't know what had suddenly come over her. She had just behaved like a ventriloquist's dummy – the words had just spilled out before she could stop them. She waited expectantly for some reaction, almost certain that he would blow a fuse; but he remained subdued.

"I also threw that old rocker in the skip outside whilst you were away, and when I came home from work it was back in the house – and I sure as hell didn't put it there. What's more, I also went upstairs to the top floor rooms and I saw a film being projected on a screen showing a family in the grounds of Juniper when it was a grand house. What's more, the boy in the film was the one who disappeared through that closed door." It had all come out so fast that she could hardly catch her breath and she wasn't sure where her nerve had come from. But there it was, the deed was done, and she felt better for it. She'd finally got it all off her chest, and now it was up to him.

He certainly reacted this time though and turned his head to her in amazement. He knew how scared she'd been from the outset, when she'd refused to go up to the top floor even with him by her side. He gawped at her, a look of incredulity on his face. Now he knew for absolutely definite that she had a major problem, she was at it again! She had definitely gone stark-raving-bonkers! Ever since they'd moved into Juniper she'd been out of control, and now without a shadow of a doubt she was beyond all hope. He jumped out of the rocker with the words still ringing in his ears that she'd thrown it in the skip; there were certain things in life that were unforgivable, and that was one of them.

"Right," he sneered. "Prove it all to me! Because if what you say is true, it should all be just the same up there now as what you say it was when you supposedly went up yourself."

Lucy didn't move. She wasn't intending going back up there, if that's what he was thinking.

But he grabbed her by the arm and dragged her out of her seat. She twisted her arm determinedly out of his grip and sat back down, holding onto the chair firmly and remaining poker-faced as if in a mummified state. He tried to pull her up again, but she managed to stay put as some unknown strength seemed to have invaded her body.

"Well that proves it then. You never went up there did you? You're lying – you wouldn't have had the guts," he scoffed.

"Well if you're so sure you're right, then prove it by pulling down that door to see what's hidden behind it. Of course if you're too scared to, then admit it," Lucy gloated, still clinging firmly onto the chair. "In fact that's your problem isn't it – you're afraid a ghost will jump out at you." Those few magic words seemed to do the trick.

Anton disappeared from the room, and after rummaging in his tool box in the hall he dashed upstairs. Within seconds he was hammering down the door. Lucy ran into the hall and looked up at the landing to see what was happening. She didn't exactly mean he should smash the door to bits, but that's what he was doing. She continued to watch him as he vented his anger on it. Within minutes he had smashed his way through. He tossed the hammer on the floor and walked inside – he stopped and gazed in awe.

He had exposed a large bedroom with one tall shuttered window to the front, and a smaller one to the side. Anton walked over and grappled with the shutters in an attempt to open them. It was difficult because they had stuck with age, and decades of undisturbed dust caught him off guard as it blasted his face. He looked around the room and was overwhelmed at what he saw. On one shaded wall hung a magnificent framed portrait of a young boy with blonde hair and blue eyes. There was a softness in his eyes which was vaguely familiar, but he quickly dismissed that from his thoughts as he was drawn to the beauty of the image. Although the face of the boy was very young, a high degree of intelligence seemed to ooze from his features, and there was an expression of superiority which the artist had also clearly captured. Anton looked for a signature and spotted one in the bottom corner which read: *Magdalena*. Anton also noticed as he moved around, that the boy's eyes seemed to follow him – a rare talent for any portrait artist to achieve, and he was captivated.

He began to uncover an array of other paintings which were leaning against one of the benches. They were all exceptional but for one. It was a portrait of a young girl who had no particular attributes that were obvious in the painting. Her features were dull and insignificant, and she seemed to stare sulkily at him from inside the frame. He covered it back up again, pondering on why anyone would want to paint such a morose child, yet marvelling at the ability of the artist to capture the mood in its true form.

Various tools, and unfinished workings in clay, were casually scattered around on the benches, along with manuals, journals, sketches, plans and various drawings, as if waiting for someone to return. But it was the multitude of tall shrouded figures which were lined up on the floor, in even rows, that lured him closer and he began to remove the covers one by one. He gasped in amazement as he excitedly undraped them all. Never in his life had he ever seen anything like it. Every single one was a magnificent marble sculpture, and he couldn't peel his eyes away from any of them; he had no idea why they were in the room locked away in such a manner. His gut feeling was that they should be in a museum, but on reflection he wondered if they could be stolen goods and had been locked away and forgotten. He tried to lift one of them, but it was too heavy, so he tipped it carefully to one side to see if he could find a marking anywhere. He spotted a signature carved into the base underneath which was hard to decipher, but he could tell that it was the same one as on the portrait. He didn't know who Magdalena was, or whether she was dead or alive, but without doubt her talent was exceptional.

He couldn't hazard a guess as to how long the room had been sealed up, or who the rightful owners of the sculptures could be; nor could he speculate on how long they had been there, or why. As he mulled it all over in his head, he had to admit it was an intriguing mystery, as was the house itself. But it was unlikely that he would ever get to the bottom of it. No doubt its history and the story behind its contents were destined to remain buried in the past; after all, the house had been empty for years.

He continued to explore each and every drawer, cupboard, nook and cranny; it was like Aladdin's cave. He walked over to a glass-fronted cabinet in which he could see a violin case, along with other interesting artefacts and pieces. He opened the door and took out the case and inspected it closely. There was a name engraved on the front. It was the same one again: *Magdalena*. There was clearly no end to her talents. Inside the case was a beautiful antique violin, which he could see was a very rare and beautiful instrument. He stroked it gently, but chose not to remove such a precious item. He closed the case and put it back in the cabinet where it belonged; he stood and gazed at it for a while, his head full of mixed emotions.

He felt very saddened by what he'd seen, as there was something quite solitary about it all. In his view, it was simple to calculate that

Magdalena's Ghost

Magdalena was clearly one of the former occupants. The fact that her belongings had remained locked in the house for such a long time, led him to believe that she was likely to have been one of the women who went mad. If she had been taken away against her will, maybe in her madness she had chosen to lock away all of her valuable works of art so that the authorities couldn't get their hands on any of it. It seemed a logical explanation to Anton, based upon the information which had been given to him by the local authority.

He stood still for a while and cast his eyes around the room, until they fell upon some fitted shelves. On the very top one he spotted a tall object covered in a piece of fabric. It was way out of reach and he had to stand on one of the benches in order to get to it. He carefully removed the cover to reveal a beautiful and very ornate clock decorated in black and gold. He had never seen anything like it in his life, and it wasn't difficult to work out that it was a very valuable antique. He scrutinised the clock face which had two dials above it. On further inspection he realised that they were settings for a variety of classical tunes. A cord to the side of the clock, when drawn, played the selected tune and Anton drew the cord for the one which had already been set. The most beautiful piece of music he had ever heard filled the atmosphere and he was mesmerised. It was haunting and melancholy, but exquisite and soothing like a lullaby. He was unable to tear himself away as he listened spellbound.

When the music reached Lucy's ears she recognised it immediately. It was the same as she had heard during the night. She ran up the stairs and stopped outside the door. Something was preventing her from going inside but she had no idea what it was, so she stood in the doorway and listened. She cast her mind back to the dream she had experienced where a beautiful woman had cradled her as a baby and mesmerised her with a beautiful soothing song – that same tune was now playing again.

When the music had finished, Anton covered the clock again and left it on the shelf. He turned to see Lucy watching from the doorway, but was immediately distracted by a gap in some boarding which had been inadequately screwed to the chimney breast. He edged his way towards it and gently squeezed his fingers behind the gap. He pulled slightly so that he could peer behind. He could just make out the outline of the mantle of an old fireplace, and in his excitement he'd completely forgotten about their earlier arguments.

"Hey Luce, look at this," he called over his shoulder.

But she wasn't for budging.

"What is it?" she called from the doorway.

"It looks like a really old fireplace that's been blocked up. I can't see it properly because it's concealed by this worktop. I'll soon have it opened up though. People used to block them up to stop the draughts coming down the chimneys when they were no longer in use."

Lucy shrugged her shoulders nonchalantly because she just didn't have Anton's insight when it came to Juniper, and anyway what was so compelling about a fireplace? It couldn't be as old as that range downstairs – that was really ancient. But there was something which did ignite her interest and that was the large amount of sculptures lined up on the floor. She just stared at them as if she couldn't believe what she was seeing, and it didn't escape Anton's notice.

"I don't know anything about sculptures but these look pretty valuable to me, and I would suspect they've been here for years without anyone knowing." Anton jumped to the ground. "Entering this room was as exciting as discovering a hidden treasure in a cave. I can't imagine why they were locked away in here. Whoever sealed up that door wanted to hide them from the world." He scratched his head in bewilderment.

"Maybe the owner didn't want anyone else to get their hands on them; or maybe the owner was a hoarder or a miser even. Or maybe the owner just died. But if, as the authorities said, the last occupants went mad, maybe one of them had a reason for blocking it all out, perhaps wanting to erase the memories. Crazy people do crazy things."

Anton turned round and stared at Lucy. It wasn't like her to proffer such a sagacious view point.

"That door could have been sealed up for a century for all we know," he responded.

"Well I think that's unlikely. Let's be honest Anton, anyone who moved here in the past would automatically want to know what was behind that door. They would have done exactly what you've done and opened it up."

"Yes you're probably right Luce. But I don't suppose we're ever going to know are we? I bet this house contains a few skeletons in the cupboard from past generations though, I'd love to uncover some of them."

He rummaged inside the final cupboard and came across a large pile of old newspapers. He gathered them all together and put them on top of a bench. He skipped through them and quickly scanned the headlines and the dates, and started to get excited.

"These old newspapers go back to the nineteen-fifties and sixties Luce. I think we might have hit on something here. It looks as if something very serious happened at Juniper in the past to have hit the headlines like this." He flicked through the pages whilst casting an eye over some of the articles to see if he could put some sense of order to it all.

"These papers are full of news concerning a family who lived here in the fifties, and there are quite a few photos too. The name Magdalena keeps cropping up…" he was trying to read and narrate at the same time. "It seems she was the sculptress, and also an artist, and a musician – of course I'd already worked that out from what I've already seen in here."

He began to gather up the newspapers. "I'll take all of these downstairs and we'll read through them at some point. It's fascinating stuff, and hopefully we'll learn a little about the history of the house too. It's really exciting."

Lucy had been taking it all in, and she hoped against hope that there would be something in those articles to throw some light on what she'd been experiencing. Maybe they would discover something in those old articles, which would put a story behind the faces that had been haunting her since the day they moved in. She had been convinced that the truth was hidden somewhere in that room, ever since the child appeared to her and disappeared through the door. Maybe the child's intention was to lead them to the newspapers – she certainly hoped so.

"I think that's enough for now Luce, we'd better get some shuteye, and to-morrow we'll see what all the news was about – I can't wait!"

He went downstairs with the newspapers piled up in his arms and left them on the dining table. They both retreated to bed, tired but stimulated with their findings, so much so that they hoped they would manage to switch off their brains sufficiently to sleep.

They both clambered into bed and Anton turned his back on Lucy. Undeterred by his lack of enthusiasm, she crawled up to him and slid her arms around his waist and buried her face into his warm body. Within minutes Anton was snoring and Lucy wrapped her legs around his and snuggled her face still deeper into his back, clinging on tightly as she made a determined effort to nod off.

Minutes later, as she was drifting off into a slumber, she was suddenly jolted back to the world of the living by the sound of music echoing hauntingly from somewhere inside the house. She listened in silence, gripping Anton's flesh without realising her nails were cutting into him. He awoke suddenly.

"Ouch! Luce, you're digging your nails in." He turned and pulled at her hands to free them from his flesh, but she was holding on firmly and didn't want to let go. She was drawing blood.

He dragged himself up and tried to force her clenched fingers open, in an attempt to drag them off his flesh.

"What are you doing, you're cutting me to shreds?" he snapped.

Lucy was shaking – the music was coming from the clock in *that* room.

"Listen," she whispered. "It's that clock it's playing that music again."

"There is no music playing, you've been dreaming! Don't start all that nonsense again I'm not in the mood. Loosen your grip you're hurting!" he demanded.

Lucy pulled herself up whilst still clinging onto him, but he forcibly removed her hold.

"You're now testing my patience beyond its normal limits!" he growled, as he flung himself over to his side of the bed dragging the bedding with him.

Lucy now exposed to the elements with no bedding to protect her, grabbed hold of the duvet and forced it from Anton's tight grip. He pulled it back again. The tug-of-war contest continued until Anton threw the whole lot on top of her and jumped out of bed.

"That's it!" he shouted. "I'm sleeping downstairs."

Within minutes he was noisily bounding down the stairs, across the hall, and into the sitting room, leaving Lucy to fend for herself alone in the bedroom. She was mortified.

She scrambled out of bed and grabbed her dressing gown and without hesitation ran down the stairs in search of Anton, at which point she noticed that the music had stopped.

He was just settling down in the old rocker for the night with the blanket wrapped round his legs, when Lucy burst into the room.

"I'm not sleeping up there on my own," she gasped, the fear evident in her face.

"And I won't be doing any sleeping at all whilst you're around!" he grumbled.

Lucy quickly settled on the chair opposite. She pulled her knees up to her arms and folded them around her legs, in an attempt to keep warm. Anton wasn't looking too pleased and she knew it. He was scowling at her, but clearly didn't intend to return upstairs. She remained quiet, hardly daring to breathe in case he accused her of disturbing him. The last thing she wanted was Anton disappearing back upstairs and leaving her alone down there to face the demons. The thought of which scared the living daylights out of her.

But soon he was snoring, while Lucy remained wide awake. She was cold, the fire was very low in the grate and was hardly throwing out any heat; and she didn't have a blanket like Anton did. She remained crouched in the chair, as the cold penetrated more and more. After a while she began to feel drowsy and her eyes started to droop, until she let out a piercing scream when she saw the shadowy image of a man standing behind Anton. She recognised him immediately as the one in the film which had been projected onto the screen upstairs – trim moustache, slim, debonair and wearing a striped blazer. Even in the darkness of the night the faint outline was identifiable, but it disappeared within seconds.

Anton jumped up in fright at the bloodcurdling sound, his face white with terror. He was feverishly turning his head and looking in all directions, unsure of what to expect. He saw Lucy scrunched up in the chair looking frantic, and then the anger began to take over once the aftermath of the sudden rush of adrenaline had kicked in. He was fuming so much that he looked as if he would explode. He glared at her, his eyeballs almost popping out of their sockets. Lucy didn't know which she feared the most – the shadowy figure of the man she'd just witnessed, or the look on Anton's face.

The silence that followed in that split second had Lucy trembling in fear, she knew she'd done it this time and there was no turning back. But that man had been there, she knew it. How on earth could she possibly explain that to Anton? She decided to keep quiet, and she cast her eyes towards the fire as if nothing had happened. Maybe he'd think he'd had a nightmare; after all, he'd been accusing her of the same thing often enough, so why not turn it on him.

"You frightened the life out of me," she cried. "You screamed out loud and woke me up. I wondered what on earth was happening." She cringed inside as she fibbed her way out of it. It was a small white lie, but it had to be done in order to calm him down before he throttled her. "You must have been having a nightmare."

She'd never been afraid of Anton before, but he was a changed man – the house had done that to him, and she no longer knew what he was capable of doing.

And for a moment he looked confused.

"I thought *you* were the one who screamed and woke *me* up. Are you sure about that?" he quizzed suspiciously.

Lucy nodded furiously but kept quiet. She watched him sit down again, knowing full well that he wasn't convinced, but at least it had pacified him for the time being. It didn't take long for him to fall asleep again, and once the snoring started she pushed her chair right up to the rocker in order to be as close to him as possible. She felt safer that way, in case anyone appeared again. And before long, she too was sound asleep.

13

LUCY AWOKE THE FOLLOWING MORNING with her body freezing cold and stiff from being hunched up in the chair. Anton was stretched out on the floor scrutinising all the newspapers which were spread out around him. He was so engrossed that he didn't even notice Lucy get out of the chair and make a brew. She was miffed that he hadn't even covered her with the blanket which he'd left casually draped on the rocker. He didn't seem to care about her at all these days, which made her long for her old Anton back even more.

"I've made a brew Anton," she called, as she brought two mugs over to the table.

Anton looked up in surprise and scrambled to his feet to join her.

"Those papers reported a lot of news about something that happened here in this house," he eagerly conveyed to her, as he drank from the hot mug. "It all happened in the fifties. I'll tell you what it's all about if you're interested."

"Of course I'm interested – why wouldn't I be?"

"Well, you've never shown much interest in the house before," he said nonchalantly. He got up and collected some of the papers, which he spread out on the table. He started to tell her what had happened, as he read through snippets of information from the ones which he felt were the most relevant.

"Apparently a family lived here in the fifties consisting of two children, a husband and wife. Magdalena, the wife, was a sculptress, an artist, and an accomplished musician. She played the violin and the piano. She was quite famous it seems, from what I've read about her in some of these reports. Her sculptures were well known and sought after all over the world, so the ones we've uncovered upstairs are evidently hers. They must be worth a fortune."

"So why would they have been hidden like that?"

"Who knows? We were told that the last two occupants went mad, and as you suggested madness makes people do bizarre things."

"Maybe it was to stop them from being stolen." Lucy suggested.

"Yes, I suppose you could be right. Now you mention it, the authorities did say an old woman lived here alone and was continually being burgled. So it would make sense to keep the valuables hidden away in the house. Anyway just listen to what I've read in these old newspapers. The husband was called Sinclair and they had two children who were called Beryl and Billy..."

"That's the name I read in the dust upstairs," she interrupted him excitedly.

He glared at her. She'd made him jump when she'd rudely interrupted him whilst he was reading something of great interest to her. The silence suddenly cut the atmosphere and he didn't need to speak – his expression said it all.

"If you're not interested I won't bother to tell you anything else. You're clearly overwrought, and maybe this information won't do the balance of your mind any good."

Lucy glared back. She may sound like an imbecile to him, but she knew what she'd seen, regardless of what he thought. Nevertheless she bit her tongue and restrained herself from reacting the way she felt. So she smiled graciously and begged him to tell her more, whilst keeping her seething thoughts to herself.

Anton continued to pick out the snippets of information which intrigued him the most.

"According to this article Billy was a gifted child. He was a musical genius from the day he could walk. But this is where it gets interesting: In nineteen-fifty-eight, the husband, Sinclair, disappeared from the house with the son, Billy, and neither of them were seen or heard of again." He looked across at Lucy, his face brimming with enthusiasm as he continued. "But a later report says that a witness from Judge Fields saw three men arrive that day in a big black car and they entered the house. They were described as: *city gents.* Two of them were seen later coming out again, and they had the boy with them. When the third man came out he was alone, the father didn't go with him. They all drove away in the car. And according to this, Magdalena and Beryl were away in London at the time, so they knew nothing of what was going on."

He picked up another paper, his face eager and excited.

"In this report it says that the three men who were seen taking Billy away, were known to the police as being part of a gambling syndicate, and it seems that Sinclair was an addicted gambler, although he preferred to call himself a 'professional gambler'. He had a reputation as a womaniser, and was living a life of luxury provided by his wife's earnings. Then there's a later edition which is really intriguing. It says that the police suspected that the boy had been abducted as payment for Sinclair's gambling debts, and then the husband absconded before the wife returned. The police had searched for the missing boy for many years, which is clear from the reports in these later editions from the nineteen-sixties. Anyway he was filed away as a missing person eventually, as they suspected he'd been taken abroad and Sinclair had scarpered, and so they gave up the search."

"So why would they take a child in payment of a debt?" Lucy just didn't get it.

"Well speculation was obviously rife according to these papers, because apparently he was worth a fortune because he was a genius. Anyway, later reports say that Magdalena went into retreat. She lived in the house as a recluse and never stepped foot outside it. She was hoping that her son Billy would eventually return, and so she never locked the door while she awaited his arrival. That would explain her being burgled. It's a pretty sad story really. She ended up in the madhouse eventually," he said nonchalantly.

"So the son didn't return, presumably?" responded Lucy as she picked up one of the newspapers to look at the photos. She stared at one of the pictures and gasped.

"You won't want to hear what I'm about to say, but this picture of the family is what I saw projected on that screen upstairs. All four of them were in the film, and that is exactly how they appeared. It's now beginning to make sense, except for one thing: why are they haunting the house, and why me and not you?"

Her ramblings were the last thing Anton wanted to hear, especially in the middle of his excitement at what he'd discovered in the papers. But Lucy was oblivious to his disapproving glare.

"It's all somehow connected with that old woman. She wants me out of the way, I'm sure of it."

Lucy seemed deep in thought for a moment, as she tried to figure it out. Her face suddenly lightened with inspiration.

"What if that old woman is Magdalena and she thinks you are Billy? Maybe she thinks you have come home and she's worried that I may take you away from her again. That would make sense wouldn't it?" She looked up at Anton and immediately saw the grave look on his face, but it didn't deter her. He had given her a bone to chew on, and she didn't intend to let go.

"If you think about it," she continued thoughtfully. "Magdalena would no longer resemble the beautiful woman she so obviously was in the photos. She would have been physically and mentally destroyed at losing a child, wouldn't she? So the old woman could easily be Magdalena. I wonder what happened to the daughter though." Lucy began to ponder once more, as her brain ticked away uncontrollably.

Anton gawped at her as if she'd lost her marbles. How many times was she going to twist and turn all the facts to suit her crazy story? Did she hate the house so much that she hoped to scare him away from it? If she did, she was mistaken. He was not going to give up the house, no matter what. He sighed in defeat. What was the point of continually arguing with her? Perhaps he would be wiser to play her little game and pretend to believe her, maybe that would shut her up and keep her quiet – but he doubted it. He gathered all the papers together and put them in a neat pile, somewhat disillusioned with her behaviour and obvious lack of interest.

"Well, we'd better eat so I can get on with my work, I've got plenty to do," he said brusquely, as he jumped up from his seat. She had just ruined the intrigue which he had been sharing with her. It had just served to set her off on her journey into madness – and quite frankly, he didn't want to know.

They both disappeared upstairs to get dressed before organising breakfast, and soon afterwards Anton was busy getting on with jobs around the house, whilst Lucy did some cleaning and tidying and preparing food for dinner. Later that day, she heard Anton disappear upstairs to begin work on the room they'd uncovered. He was keen to get it sorted because it was now minus a door. He wanted to move the sculptures into somewhere safe while he removed the worktop which was blocking the fireplace. He was up there for hours. Lucy went up to see how he was getting on.

"How long do you intend to work up here?" she asked, as she peered into the room. He had already moved the sculptures into an empty bedroom and had started to remove the paintings.

"It's a big job. Those sculptures weighed a ton," he replied, wiping the perspiration from his forehead. "I'm moving these paintings out of here too, so they don't get damaged when I start knocking things about." He stopped for a breather.

"I've got dinner ready."

Magdalena's Ghost

"Oh that's good to hear, I'm famished. I'll just take these last ones into the other room and I'll be down in a jiffy."

Lucy went back down to serve their meal, and the smell of food as Anton walked into the room made his mouth water. He sat down eagerly at the table rubbing his hands with glee. He had worked up a healthy appetite.

They ate in silence, and Lucy brooded over the uncomfortable situation between them which had only materialised since they moved into the house. He clearly wasn't going to believe anything that had gone on, nor would he believe her if anything else happened. She couldn't understand. It wasn't so difficult to take on board, after all, everyone had read, or heard about ghosts from time to time, whether they believed in them or not. Surely he could safely presume that if she'd seen them with her own eyes, it was evidence enough that they existed. But deep down she knew that he didn't want to believe, because he didn't want to believe in anything that would spoil his loving relationship with Juniper.

She was lost in her thoughts, as another pattern emerged which was beginning to make sense. If that old woman was the ghost of Magdalena as she had speculated, the distress and anguish of losing her son in the fifties, coupled with the life she must have lived as a recluse thereafter, would have undoubtedly taken its toll both physically and mentally. And if she'd waited in vain for him to come home for the remaining years of her life, maybe after she'd died her spirit had carried on inside Juniper and continued to wait for Billy's return. The more she dwelt on it, the more convinced she was that this time she may well have just hit on the right scenario. It all somehow made sense.

But what about the child who she now realised was Billy? Why had he shown himself? Was he trying to communicate with her? And why did he disappear through that door? And if his spirit was haunting Juniper too, wouldn't the old woman know he was there? If she did, and they were together, what would be the point of their spirits remaining in the house?

With those thoughts in mind, she had somewhat annihilated her earlier convictions and she was back to square one. And then there was the question of the daughter. Where did she figure in it all? Her mind was in turmoil again, it all began to swim around in her head until it ached. She shouldn't be sharing this alone Anton should be on her side. After all it was his idea to buy the house. How could she ever win him back if he refused to listen or do something about it?

It all seemed so impossible to her and it made her feel saddened.

She looked up at Anton as he cleared the last morsels of food from his plate. She still loved him, regardless of anything else. He looked exactly the same – nothing had changed in that sense. But he had become someone else inside. Was she ever going to be able to turn the clock back, or change what had passed between them these last few months? Was it too late to rectify the damage that had been done? She didn't have the answers, nor was she sure if she had sufficient stamina to keep on trying. She was in a very lonely place right now – and she was in it alone.

Anton shoved his plate aside and got up from the table.

"I'll get cracking again Luce. No point wasting precious time, there's plenty left to do up there."

"Surely you're not going to try to do everything this evening?"

"I'll just keep on until I can't do any more." He disappeared out of the room and went back upstairs. Soon he was hammering and banging again, and Lucy left him to it. How tedious life had become since Juniper. And as she reflected on the current situation, she couldn't help but wonder if it mirrored the rest of their lives together. Could it be that all they had to look forward to from now on was work, work and even more work? She felt downhearted and depressed.

She reached across for the pile of newspapers and casually flipped through them. She began to read some of the reports and just as Anton had said the news had really hit the headlines. Apparently the daughter abandoned Magdalena in the early sixties and so she continued to live alone in Juniper. Lucy shivered as she thought about the implications of it all, and the similarity to how she'd felt herself when she'd been on her own in the house when Anton was away. It must have been even worse for Magdalena as she waited tirelessly and relentlessly for her son's return, possibly never knowing what had happened to him, or whether he was dead or alive. It didn't bear thinking about, and it certainly didn't help to improve Lucy's feelings towards the house either. She felt desperately sorry for Magdalena as she visualised the life she'd clearly had, which was evident in the film upstairs and the newspapers. She'd been a beautiful and sophisticated woman with an infectious smile, and in the film she'd looked deliriously happy as she played with her young son.

To think that such a talented woman with independent means, could be so badly treated by the cad of a husband as was described in the news reports, was hard to digest. She should have grown old with her family around her, a family who she had supported, cared for and provided for. But instead she was driven to madness through despair, sorrow and tragedy. Lucy couldn't help but wonder what had happened to the husband eventually. He must have scarpered pretty fast while Magdalena and the daughter were away in London after what he'd done. She had read that mother and daughter were in London because Beryl, the daughter, was auditioning for a place in a world famous ballet school, and if that version was in fact true, it highlighted what a talented family they must have been. Pity the husband couldn't lay claim to any talent other than gambling; he had obviously been the ruin of them all. And what did really happen to Billy? Did he survive the years that followed? Or did the trauma he must have clearly suffered at the loss of his dear, sweet and loving mother cut short his young and innocent life? Did his amazing talents remain with him wherever he went, or were they lost to the world from that moment on? Or was it remotely possible that his genius stayed behind in Juniper? One thing for sure, they were never going to know now. It was an old, forgotten story, a story full of myths and speculation which had long since been confined to those archived files labelled *unsolved crimes* – that is if a crime had indeed ever been committed.

Lucy couldn't imagine a father giving away his son, as it was not in her psyche to think that way. She believed that children were born out of love. Maybe he didn't have a choice. If a set of gangsters took the child as was rumoured, he might have had no say in the matter and then took off before his wife returned because he couldn't face her. Maybe he had taken his own life; after all he didn't seem to have had one without Magdalena. If he had no other means of support, he too would have faced ruin. That made it even sadder than ever in Lucy's mind, as she thought of an entire family being destroyed by one man's foolishness. But of course who's to say that any of it was true? And who's to say they didn't return? The papers may well have forgotten about the whole saga and even lost interest, in their pursuit of newer, more tantalising news.

By now she had worn her brain out and she didn't want to do any more thinking. It was tiring and had muddled her mind. She was probably more confused now, than before reading the newspaper reports. Prior to those it had all seemed much simpler – that the house was haunted and they should sell up and leave. She breathed a deep sigh, as the weight on her shoulders now seemed even heavier to bear.

As the evening drew close Anton continued to work in the room upstairs. He had emptied it of all its valuables, including the violin, and stored them elsewhere for safekeeping. He had removed the worktops, most of which were only connected by brackets, and piled them neatly together against a wall with the intention of making use of them somewhere else later. He stopped to have a rest while he stood and admired the fireplace, which seemed to be all intact although evidently not used for some time. He walked over to inspect it more closely and noticed that it appeared to have been fastened to the wall with a couple of eyelet brackets to the sides. He thought it strange, because it was obvious to him that it was very old and had been there for a very long time – probably as long as the house. And it wouldn't have been screwed to the wall in such a flimsy way originally. On closer observation, he also discovered that it was only very loosely connected to the wall. He pulled on it to see if it moved, but it was so heavy that its weight alone would have held it in place. He therefore concluded that it had been removed at some time or another and refitted, albeit in an inappropriate manner. His curiosity aroused, he picked up his tools again and began to unscrew the fasteners carefully. He hesitated, knowing full well that it would weigh a ton and it must have taken more than one man to remove it and put it back again. There must have been some essential work required to the chimney breast for the need to remove the fireplace. But it wasn't level, he'd noticed, and so he decided it needed to come out in order for him to refit it properly.

It unscrewed quite easily, but he had a dilemma on his hands. How was he going to remove it on his own? It was cast iron, and Lucy wasn't strong enough, or big enough, to be of assistance, so he took the gamble and proceeded to pull it loose on his own. He inched it out of the opening bit by bit, until the gap was just wide enough to see behind. It was quite stable as its weight kept it upright, and so far as he could see it was all in one piece. He picked up a torch from his tool box and shone it into the space behind. He couldn't see much at first, until his eyes grew accustomed to the dark and finally fell upon what looked to be a roll of carpet along with a load of junk. He inched the fireplace out a little more, but the weight had him beat and he knew he'd moved it as far as he was able to on his own. He had, however, managed to move it sufficiently to squeeze his body behind. It was tight, but there was sufficient space for him to examine the brickwork with his torch, as well as the rubbish that had been left behind. He presumed that someone had sealed up the chimney at one time or another, and dropped all the rubble down the chimney breast beforehand, which was normal practice to some builders.

But very soon he was squeezing his body back out again. He left the fireplace in the same position knowing it was stable enough for the time being. He very quickly put some of the worktops together and made a make-shift door with which to block the entrance, in an attempt to temporarily seal off the room again. He went downstairs to find Lucy, who was busy unpacking some of the boxes which were still in the hall.

"Shall we have a brew Luce?" he asked, as he walked past her and towards the sitting room.

She followed him willingly, glad that he'd finally come down but quick to notice the seriousness in his voice. She knew he'd been working far too hard, and the consistent labour without the benefits of breaks to abate the monotony, was not good for the soul.

"I'll do it," she offered, as she made her way to the scullery. "You sit down and have a rest." She pointed to the old rocker which was in its usual place in front of the fire. She wanted to be on her best behaviour after all he'd been working jolly hard and the last thing he would feel like doing was listening to her and her normal rantings.

Anton was deep in thought as he sat down and stared into the fire. He had a lot of explaining to do to Lucy and he didn't know just where to start. She soon returned with two mugs of tea and some cake and sat down opposite.

"I built the fire up because it had gone very cool," she said, as she warmed her hands on the hot mug.

Anton didn't reply. He looked at her and for the first time saw the tiredness etched in her face. Lines which had never been there before were now visible across her forehead and around her eyes. He watched her gazing silently into the fire as she tried to warm her small hands on the large mug, and he reflected on how little she smiled these days. He remembered clearly how she used to laugh until she cried, and how light hearted they both used to feel as they enjoyed their simple and uncluttered life together. They'd had no worries, no problems and they were happy, and could only have envisaged a bright future ahead of them. In those days life was fun. But he had failed her. He knew that now.

He drank his tea as he remained engrossed in his thoughts. It didn't escape Lucy's notice but she had grown weary with the arguments, and his sullen expression only encouraged her to remain silent. She could hardly say anything these days without it spurring Anton into action, which often resulted in a full-blown row.

But several minutes later Anton jumped up.

"I have to go out," he said, without explanation.

Lucy jumped up too, not wanting to be left alone in the house. The evening had grown dark, and it was a time when strange things seemed to happen whenever she was alone in Juniper.

"I'll come with you," she said eagerly.

But her expectations of escaping the boredom of being indoors, as well as the fear of any unexplained visits, were dashed to a pulp when Anton told her to stay where she was as he disappeared without explanation. She was miffed when she heard him drive off. She had no idea where he was going, or why, and once again she felt the pain of being excluded from his life. What was so important that he didn't have time to explain? She couldn't understand why he was behaving in such a manner, but by now it was becoming commonplace and she simply had no choice but to put up with it – at least for now. But she was tired and weary with everything and if she couldn't resolve the problems between them, she would have to take a serious look at their future together.

14

Anton didn't return for two hours, by which time Lucy was frantic. She ran to the door when she heard his van pull up, but as she opened it she saw a police car drive into the grounds and park behind him. She rushed outside to see what was wrong, but Anton ushered her into the house and told her to go back to the sitting room and wait for him.

He led two policemen upstairs, and as she stood in the hall below she watched them remove the barricade from the room where Anton had been working. She remained there for a while, listening and wondering what on earth was going on. She could hear some shifting and bumping and muffled voices from within the room, but she couldn't fathom out what was happening. Unless, of course, they were removing the valuable sculptures and artefacts which had been discovered, which would make sense. She retreated back into the sitting room, and went into the scullery to boil the kettle in case they all wanted a brew. But several minutes later Anton bounded into the room and told her to get organised for the two of them to spend a few days in the camper van. He informed her that as the early season had begun, they were going to spend some time in their favourite village and he'd explain everything on the way.

Obviously Lucy was delighted and could hardly believe it, but she knew something was wrong and she didn't know what – but she didn't intend to rock the boat. Keeping shtum was the best thing she could do in the circumstances. She hurriedly gathered the bare essentials together and piled it all in the van, whilst Anton checked that everything downstairs in the house was safe to leave. They were gone within minutes, but the police stayed behind. Although Lucy was puzzled about the entire situation, she knew that Anton would get round to explaining it eventually.

Over the next forty-eight hours Judge Fields was a hive of activity and speculation was rife, as police cordoned off access to the property and labelled it as a crime scene. Residents peered out of their windows, and others wandered up to the house to see if they could find out what was happening; but information was not forthcoming. Camera crews lined Gallows Lane, most of which camped out in the hope that they would be the first to discover what had happened. But some canny reporters had investigated the history of Juniper House and put two and two together when they'd discovered the disappearance of Magdalena's husband and son. Whilst they could only speculate on what was going on inside the house, they were confident enough to spill the beans on their own theories and speculations, which served only to get the village tongues wagging no end. Some reports said that the husband and son had been found buried in the grounds, others speculated that they had been found in a cellar. Some of the residents gossiped about the couple who had recently moved in, as they speculated on where they had disappeared to; concluding that they had been arrested for some heinous crime.

In the meantime Anton and Lucy had booked in at a campsite in their favourite village, and although the weather was still quite chilly there was plenty of sunshine, so they were able to do lots of walking before ending up at the local pub each day.

Anton had explained to Lucy that he had discovered what appeared to be human remains wrapped in a roll of carpet, which had been concealed behind the fireplace. Neither of them wanted to speculate on what, or who it was. He'd been shocked when he first discovered it, and had to think long and hard at what to do. He didn't tell Lucy immediately after the grizzly find, as he didn't want to unnerve her any more than necessary. So he had temporarily blocked the room up and chosen to report it to the police first, to see what they would do about it.

Lucy had remained silent about it all, but she had her own theories influenced by the bizarre incidents she had experienced in the house. It was now evident, as far as she was concerned, that when the child appeared to her before disappearing through the door, he was trying to lead her to the truth of what had happened to him – and perhaps his father – all those years ago. There was no doubt in her mind that the skeletal remains would prove to be the boy. Maybe the father had killed him? Maybe the three men had never existed, apart from in the mind of some villager wanting to get in on the act? Or maybe they were both murdered and concealed behind the fireplace; only time would tell when the police finished their investigations. And then the horror of Magdalena's plight came to the forefront of her mind. That poor woman! Living alone in the house for all those years not knowing that her beloved child lay dead in that horrible room – and even maybe the husband! What did Magdalena know? Did she know anything at all? Was she perhaps a witness to what went on – or maybe, even maybe, she was involved in some way? Then her thoughts went to Beryl. Nothing seemed to exist in the history of Juniper involving Beryl. She had seemingly disappeared too. Was she involved? And who sealed up the room? Was it to hide all the valuable sculptures, works of art and artefacts? Or was it something more sinister – perhaps to stop the bodies from ever being discovered? Her head began to ache again as she wore her brain out with her speculations and theories once more. She wasn't much of a detective really, and never had been, so trying to work it all out had made her feel sick and dizzy. Of course there was nothing to prove that the body, or bodies, or parts, had anything to do with Magdalena's past – they could be completely unrelated; maybe even more skeletal remains of a pet, or pets. She didn't want to dwell on it any more, as it was all far too stressful and too complicated.

She wasn't sure what they would do now. If the skeletal remains turned out to be human ones, and as yet no-one was prepared to say, then surely they couldn't return to the house after their gruesome discovery, and knowing what had happened there sometime in the past? But where would they go? They couldn't live in the camper van. The questions in her mind were endless, but that's where they would have to remain for the time being because she didn't intend to spoil their idyllic moments together.

They took advantage of their desperately needed time together in a more relaxed and pleasurable environment, and within a couple of days they were both feeling de-stressed. Anton had been deep in thought, and not much conversation had passed between them. But they were both safe in the knowledge that the longer they stayed away from Juniper, and its influences, the more their feelings for one another were being rejuvenated. Lucy felt that her old Anton was slowly coming back into view, and the forces which had held him in their spell during the time they lived in the house, were gradually being drained away. It was like old times again, nothing had changed. They were both the same carefree people once more, just enjoying the simple things they had in common, and treasuring each other's company. Without the strong influence of material wealth being worn around their necks like a ball and chain, they were free to discover each other all over again. And this time Lucy didn't intend to let him go.

Five days had passed and neither of them wanted to think about returning home, because home is what it was and that was something they could not escape from. But Anton had been making plans in his mind as to what he thought they should do. One evening as they both lay in bed listening to the stirring of the wind beating gently against the side of the van, he spoke:

"I've been thinking Luce," his voice serious.

Lucy looked up at him, a swift moment of fear in her eyes as she thought he was going to tell her something that she wouldn't want to hear.

"I think we should put Juniper back on the market for sale." He waited for her reaction, but she was too surprised to take it in.

"I can finish what I started. I know I can get the house decent enough to interest buyers, and in the meantime I think we should see if our old flat is still available."

Lucy sat up in bed and stared at him, unable to believe her ears.

"What's made you decide that all of a sudden?"

"I don't want you going back to Juniper. It's over, finished, there's nothing there for us and I now realise that there never was. I've been giving it a lot of thought whilst I've been free of its influences." He pulled her to him and slipped his arm around her. "I don't how to begin saying I'm sorry for the beastly way I've treated you. Somehow that house put a spell on me. I felt as if I were someone else. It was almost as if a stranger had inhabited my head and I was no longer in control of my thoughts or actions. I can't explain it Luce, but I now feel as if I've been untethered, set free as it were. My mind is now clear and it's been made up. We're getting out of there Luce; my first responsibility is to you. I took us there and it's up to me to make sure I get us out of it, before our relationship is destroyed altogether. No-one is to blame but me."

He held her in a strong hug and kissed her tenderly. Lucy was reeling with happiness and joy, and the relief was something she couldn't put into words; but she knew that words weren't necessary. He had obviously realised how she'd been feeling and that was all that mattered. Her old Anton was back and she was happy for him to take control. He was always right in the end, and whatever decisions he made she knew would be for the good of them both.

"But what if our old flat has been taken?" she asked hesitantly.

"We're not exactly homeless, so if it's not available I'm sure something else will be. I know it will be hard going for a while, that is until we sell Juniper. But we should come out with some profit if I work hard to get it looking good, and I can work there of an evening and at week-ends. We'll find something, I know we will."

They clung to one another as they slept in each other's arms. Lucy knew that in time they would be able to rub out the past events of Judge Fields and put it all behind them. One day it would be a forgotten story, and their happiness would be set in stone. She could put all her faith and confidence in whatever Anton chose to do, because once more he was her rock and she adored him.

The first thing they did when they set off back, was to call in at the agent's office to see if they had any properties on their books which they could move into fairly quickly; and they were both elated when they were told that their old flat was available. Without hesitation the agent gave them the keys and told them that they would draw up a lease in the next day or two, while they got the flat organised with utilities etc. Lucy kept pinching herself to make sure she was awake and not the victim of a cruel dream. When they arrived back home, the police had gone and there was little evidence of them having been there, apart from the carpet and its contents having been removed. As there was little or no change in Juniper, they both decided that they would remain in the house for at least a week or two, in order to pack up and get everything sorted in readiness for their move back to the flat. Anton promised her he would not leave her in the house alone again, and with him by her side Lucy had no problem with the arrangement.

A week later Anton called in to see the police and he was told that the remains were at least fifty to sixty years old, and possibly more. They had been easily identified by items of clothing, jewellery and dental records, as those of Magdalena's husband. They could confirm that he had been stabbed to death and they had found the weapon wrapped in the bundle with the skeletal remains.

The police had been able to check their archives and had discovered in the records that Sinclair and the boy had gone missing in nineteen-fifty-eight, but with no suspicious circumstances. The boy was presumed to be with the father who had deserted his wife and daughter. Back in the fifties it would not necessarily have been considered a crime, as the husband's rights would outweigh those of the wife. Therefore the records were filed away and closed. If indeed the rumours had been true, that there had been three men seen by villagers to enter the house and remove the child, there was absolutely nothing they could do about it now, it was too long ago and they would all be dead. Maybe they did take the child abroad, as was rumoured, and maybe he lived out his life with a good family somewhere. There was even a chance he could still be alive, after all he would be just another old man by now; but the bottom line was – no-body cared. It didn't matter to anyone in their jurisdiction, so as far as they were concerned that was the end of it. It was another closed book.

Anton and Lucy knew that none of it was their responsibility. They had bought the house, not its past, and sometimes the past is best forgotten. They had concluded that when the police removed the body, they had removed the silent stirrings of evil which had remained within its walls, undisturbed, until they had moved in.

There was only one thing left to do in order to rid it of its tragic past. They had both agreed to donate the sculptures, and other valuables, to a charity for the protection of children to be auctioned for their benefit. Magdalena, surely, would have been happy with that and should rest more peacefully in her grave wherever that might be. They both believed that they had been drawn to Juniper for a reason that day. It was destiny that they had to move there in order to uncover the tragic events of so long ago, so that its spirits could finally rest in peace. Whilst they could never know the answer, they believed that they were the chosen ones who could enter that world and come out at the other end unscathed. Their job was done, and now it was time for them to move on and get on with their own lives. And whilst Lucy knew that there were still many pieces missing from the jigsaw, they were happy to walk away; their life together in the future was more important than something buried in the past.

Somehow Magdalena had been caught up in a time-warp where everything had simply stood still; it happened when she was alive and again after she'd died. All that time she had spent her days waiting for

Billy, something she'd never been able to come to terms with. Knowing her husband to be a bounder, and having her own private earnings, his loss would seem inconsequential in comparison to that of her beloved son. Probably in her mind her husband had stolen him away from her, and her hope was that one day Billy would, of his own accord, find his way back to the loving home he had known with his mother. But it was Billy's spirit which had returned as a child to guide Lucy to the truth of what had happened to his father; in her view he had to have known about it. But the one thing that puzzled her was why he hadn't led her to the truth of where he, as a child, had gone on that fatal day in nineteen-fifty-eight. Perhaps the rumours were true, that he had been taken abroad and kept by the people whose debts the father could not repay. It was a tragic story involving cruelty and treachery by the very persons Magdalena had loved, trusted and cared for.

The police, meanwhile, had their own theory. They believed that when Magdalena and Beryl went off to London, the men who had been witnessed by the residents of Judge Fields had seized the opportunity and taken the boy out to their car while they killed the father. They no doubt discovered that Sinclair did not have the money to pay what he owed. They will have taken the boy away before returning to clean up and conceal the body behind the fireplace, knowing it was unlikely to ever be discovered. They had, from all reported facts, disappeared without trace and it was therefore presumed they had gone abroad with the boy. They thought it unlikely that the boy had been murdered, if, as it was rumoured, they had taken him in payment of the debt.

Apparently it was also rumoured that Magdalena had ordered workmen to seal up the door in order to protect her valuable works of art. Because she continually left the door unlocked for her son to return, she became the victim of many break-ins, whereby most of her contents were removed. Later investigations had revealed that Magdalena had made a will in favour of Billy, in case he returned after her death. He was to have the house and its contents, and the sculptures would have given him security for the remaining years of his life.

But Beryl had cheated Billy out of his inheritance and had committed the cruellest of crimes against her vulnerable mother; and when she'd abandoned her at a time when she needed support, surely she must have known in her warped mind that she had disinherited herself from the estate. Magdalena, however, when she'd had the door sealed up, might well have known, or guessed that Beryl would return one day. Perhaps she wasn't as mad as everyone thought. By hiding away the valuables, she had succeeded in tricking Beryl to believing that everything of value, including the amazing antique musical clock, had been stolen. At least she didn't reap the benefit of her mother's incredible talents and hard work, and therefore Magdalena had outwitted her in the end.

Magdalena would have had no idea that her husband's body had been sealed up behind the fireplace, and her deteriorating frame of mind, over the years, would allow her memory only to be penetrated by the loss of Billy. Living there alone she would have gradually been forgotten, and curiosity from the villagers would eventually die with them. When the daughter returned all those years later, no doubt prompted by the rumours that the old lady had *lost it*, she seized the opportunity to take what she believed was rightfully hers. There was no-one to question her actions, therefore the crimes all went unpunished and unsolved. Poor Magdalena, Lucy thought, she didn't deserve what she went through – what a tragic story of events.

Anton and Lucy had one more night to stay at Juniper, and the following morning they would move all of their belongings back to the flat. They decided to have an early night in readiness for an early start the next day.

Anton checked that everything was secure before joining Lucy who had already settled down in bed for a good night's sleep. They cuddled up together, happy in the knowledge that soon they would be back where they belonged. It took no time at all for them both to nod off.

During the course of the early hours, the sound of music could be heard in the distance and Lucy was the first one to wake up to it. She sat up in bed and concentrated to make sure she wasn't hearing imaginary sounds. But she knew without doubt that she could hear the piano playing a beautiful but melancholy tune; she recognised it as the same tune as on the musical clock.

"Anton, wake up," she whispered, as she rocked him and shook him until he opened his eyes.

"Huh? What's wrong?" his words were slurred as he tried to wake up.

"Listen, can't you hear it, it's that music again."

Anton sat up and listened until the musical notes eventually reached his ears.

"Where's it coming from?" he asked, still groggy from having been forced awake.

"Someone's playing the piano downstairs."

At that moment Anton seemed to wake up with a start. He jumped out of bed, and Lucy followed as he stopped at the door. He took a deep breath and stealthily opened it. He walked out onto the landing and listened. Lucy joined him.

"It sounds like it's from downstairs," he whispered. "You wait here and I'll go down and take a look. I'll get the hammer out of my tool box."

"What for?" exclaimed Lucy looking at him, and wondering if perhaps he wasn't really awake after all.

"In case it's a burglar, that's what for," he answered, puzzled as to why she should question his actions.

"You don't need a hammer to protect you from ghosts. They won't do you any harm."

He looked at her questioningly, and after grabbing his dressing gown he proceeded to go downstairs with Lucy following close behind. He made sure he retrieved the hammer from his tool box in the hall on the way through. The music was coming from the sitting room and he felt a cold shiver run down his spine. But Lucy was unfazed. She was no longer afraid.

Anton stopped dead in his tracks as he recognised the old man sitting at the piano playing like a master of music. Lucy stood beside Anton and grabbed his arm to stop him going any further. She held onto him tightly, as they both watched and listened. The music was mesmerising, and the silence of the house in the dead of night further enhanced the beautiful sounds. Neither of them had ever heard, or experienced, anything so beautiful before and they didn't want it to end. The only distraction a few minutes later was the old woman coming from the scullery and entering the room. She walked slowly towards the piano as if in a trance, but the most amazing and incomprehensible thing of all was what followed. As she approached the piano, the old man began to change into a small and delicate child of around six-years-old. He had blonde hair and small features, and he continued to play the masterpiece uninterrupted. The old lady began to change too, and they witnessed her transition from the old ragged person she had become, to a beautiful, elegant and sophisticated young woman. Holding a violin at her side, she moved towards the piano as if floating on air. Her smile was radiant and her loveliness captivating. Anton and Lucy became awestruck with her beauty and the accomplishments of them both, as she began to play to the magnificent sounds being produced by the hands of the genius child.

They both listened in silence as if rooted to the spot, unwilling and unable to move, knowing that they were privileged to share those rare and precious moments between mother and son.

Anton slid his hand into Lucy's, his body trembling with emotion at what they were seeing. Lucy didn't feel any fear at all, in fact the emotions from Magdalena seemed to flood her mind and the happiness spread throughout her whole being.

When the music ended, it was followed by the most unimaginable experience they could ever have thought possible. The child slipped his hand into his mother's, and together they walked from the room and disappeared through the closed door of the entrance hall and out of the house altogether. It was as if Anton and Lucy did not exist in their world and never could have.

For a while, neither of them could speak. It was as if the story had reached its climax and all had been revealed to them in those few precious moments. Magdalena had found her child. He had returned, who knows when, or how, but they were clearly together in spirit. Their visit was intended to show the young couple how their story had ended, and to let them know that they would have no need to return again to the memories of the past. The house was finally rid of its ghosts, its presences, its mysteries and there was nothing more to be feared. Although the jigsaw was incomplete as far as Anton and Lucy were concerned, the last page of the story had been turned and read. And as far as any missing pages were concerned they would have to invent their own version.

15

Everything was packed up and stacked into the Transit van which they'd hired. Lucy jumped in beside Anton, and as they drove out of the grounds Lucy glanced back for a few seconds, just sufficient time for her to whisper: "*Goodbye Magdalena.*"

She had to admit to a brief moment of sadness as they disappeared out of Judge Fields and onto the main road which took them back to their former home. Anton had showed no emotion whatsoever, he seemed relieved as if a burden had been taken from his shoulders. But Lucy felt that she would be leaving a little piece of fondness behind in Juniper, primarily because she had experienced some very strong emotional tugs during their time there, and particularly when the boy had appeared before her. That final visit from Magdalena, as she would have been when the boy disappeared, and the vision of her as she declined into old age and despair, would stay with Lucy for a long time, possibly the rest of her life. She felt enormously privileged to have witnessed the traumatic life of such a talented and amazing woman, which had been cut short by a tragedy which had turned her into an aged and mentally-unstable recluse. She took away with her a strong piece of emotion which she felt would be hard to shake off for many years to come, or perhaps even never.

Lucy had grown up during their time at Judge Fields, she had learned that life was not meant to be a bed of roses and that nothing could remain perfect forever; and she intended to learn from that experience to help make her a better and more unselfish person. Before Juniper, she had doted on Anton without feeling that she should make more effort, convinced that what they shared could not be tested, or dented in any way, and she had taken it all for granted. But she was wrong, Juniper had proven that. Her love for Anton was much stronger and deeper than before, because it had grown into something more meaningful, and she knew that Anton felt the same. She'd heard many times that love would either deepen, or fall apart, during the test of time, and it was important to shake off the fantasies of youth and to accept those changes if they wanted it to survive. She now understood that in its true context. They had both moved into Juniper House as a naïve pair of romantics – just a boy and a girl. But they moved out as man and woman, both of them much wiser and stronger and their relationship much more stable.

Over the next month or two, Anton worked hard on getting the house ready for selling. The estate agents had suggested they put it up for sale immediately, while he carried out the necessary work. Much to his surprise the house sold quickly, so he had to put extra hours in to get the work done. As expected, the new purchasers wanted to install their own kitchen and bathrooms, and that cut out a lot of work for Anton as he put the finishing touches to what he'd already done.

Anton continually passed through Judge Fields as he went back and forth to the house, and on one occasion he noticed a large banner had been draped across the front of the old pub, which read: *Opening soon - under new management*. He didn't think too much about it apart from his mind drifting back to the old man – the one he saw reappear in the house. None of it made sense to him, and he just couldn't understand the connection to the boy or the woman. He'd always presumed the old man was dead after he failed to appear again in the pub, and he'd presumed the pub had just closed for the winter months, not for good. But he didn't allow himself to dwell on it for long, as it was too complicated as far as he was concerned. In his view Lucy was too emotional about such things. She had a habit of allowing them to take over her mind, which then became over-imaginative. He thought it better to forget the whole thing and that's what he'd done.

The closure of the sale came soon enough. Anton had completed the necessary work which he'd promised to do before exchange of contracts, and the purchasers, a couple with three children, were delighted.

On the week of completion, he'd suggested to the agents and solicitors that he would leave the keys behind the bar of the old pub, which he'd noticed when passing had re-opened. He hadn't been inside it since they had moved into Juniper, and it felt somewhat strange, although familiar, when he walked into the bar area. The new landlord was standing behind the bar drying some pint glasses. He greeted him on entry with a beaming smile.

"Hello son, what can I do for you?"

"I'm from Juniper up the road. I've just sold it and I wonder if I can leave the keys here for the new owners. It'll give them a chance to get to know somebody at least, before they move in."

"Aye, you're right there lad. Yon house is a bit hidden up there behind all those trees, in fact hardly anyone passing would know it's there if they're not from the village."

"Well we came across it accidentally I must admit."

"Spent some time doing it up, have you?" he asked, while he continually dried a pint glass to a shine.

"Yes, it's been hard work but worth it."

"As long as you make a profit, that's all that matters. Property developer are you?" he quizzed.

"I'll have a glass of lager please."

The barman served him with the drink and walked over to the till to deposit the money. Anton looked wistfully across the bar to where the old man used to stand.

"No, I'm not a developer," he finally answered as he sipped his drink. "What happened to the last landlord, I didn't realise he'd left?"

The man looked at him curiously. "A bit before your time I would have thought young man. This place hasn't been occupied for tens of years."

Anton looked at him, presuming he didn't know about the last landlord.

"I came in a few months ago and …"

"The only people who could have been here would be surveying the place," he interrupted. "They would either be from the brewery, or maybe their workmen. But I can tell you, on authority, that it's been closed for years."

Anton was convinced that the barman didn't know what he was talking about, especially if he didn't come from the area.

"I know it was pretty dead when we came, so it's no surprise that it closed down, I never saw any customers."

The barman peered back at him.

"I was born and bred in Judge Fields, son. I left the area a long time ago to work away, but I knew Old Jim Thorney. He was the last landlord to run this place and it was years ago. I used to pop in for a pint whenever I visited my old mother, during her decline. He was much older than me, been dead for years. In fact he went to school with a lad from Juniper House, come to think of it. Only primary school, mind you, because the lad was only young when he went missing. I wasn't even born then. But my old mum told me all about it – she knew all what went on around here you know. It was a bit of a scandal at the time from what she used to tell me."

Anton was confused. He knew he was not mistaken, because even though the pub had evidently been refurbished, the layout and the bar were the same. He let the barman continue without interrupting him.

"He came back you know."

"Who came back?"

"Billy – yes, that's what they called the boy ... it was Billy. He was an old man when he returned, not in years but in stature and appearance. He'd had a hard life you see."

"What happened to him?" Anton was now keenly curious, although somewhat bemused.

"He was only six years old when he was taken away by some men. He never really knew why though, he was too young to understand back then. Something to do with his father owing them money is what he said. He was taken abroad, but he managed to get away in his teens and he went to sea. He'd clearly suffered from his life as a seafaring- man, it showed in his face and his stature. Pity when you knew what his background was and where he'd come from."

Anton had nothing to say. He didn't understand really, and was still of a mind to believe the landlord had got his facts wrong about the closure of the pub. He let him continue.

"By the time I was old enough to hear about the scandal, his mother – Magdalena I think she was called – had gone into decline. I was only a boy and didn't really understand what it was all about. But the villagers who'd known her before the incident, had said she used to be a beautiful woman and very highly regarded, but her husband was a cad."

"What happened to Billy when he came back?"

"He stayed here, in this pub. Old Jim let him stay because the daughter – I guess that was Billy's sister Beryl – had taken over Juniper. It was common knowledge that Magdalena had left the house to Billy in case he ever returned – apparently she always knew he would one day. It was written into her will. She evidently wasn't too mad to do that! But then I guess she probably did it soon after he'd disappeared, maybe before her mind was gone. She probably wanted to make sure her husband didn't get anything, knowing his reputation. It was a sad affair really. She was a wrong 'un you know – the daughter, that is. They reckon she took after the father. She robbed Magdalena blind, took everything she owned including the house which she fraudulently possessed. And she managed to get Magdalena sectioned, after transferring the house into her own name. Sad thing was that Magdalena never knew that Billy had come back, and it was all she'd ever waited for. But she was in the madhouse by then, and Beryl was well and truly ensconced in Juniper."

They were both silent for a while, the barman deep in thought as Anton sipped at his drink waiting to hear more, although unable to digest the facts in an intelligible way.

"Nobody knew he was back apart from the landlord," he continued. "And me of course, although I sure didn't tell anyone. No point feeding a village full of gossipers with idle talk, and besides, he didn't want anyone to know, including his sister. He used to stand over there." He pointed across the bar. "Over in yon corner, with his half-empty glass on the counter top. Long white hair, unshaven and unkempt but for the shoes he wore. He always had a shine on his shoes did Billy."

Anton felt a cold shiver run down his spine.

"Oh yes, and he had manicured nails as well, I remember that. And long elegant fingers, even though they were riddled with arthritis. Pianist hands you might say, because that's what he did as a boy. And I know something else too." The landlord grinned at Anton mischievously.

"And what's that?" asked Anton, all ears listening.

"He had a set of keys to Juniper. Apparently the daughter came in here a few times like a raving lunatic. He walked her back to the house a couple of times, so I heard, and he picked up a set which he'd seen hanging in the hall. It must have been a difficult experience for him, although he'd hardly remember it I suppose. But he must have had *some* memories of his childhood there. Imagine going back after all those years and finding it in that condition. From all accounts, it had deteriorated beyond recognition. The keys were possibly his last hope of holding onto something of his past, for what it was worth. The authorities seized the house you see, they took it to pay for the asylum fees. So Billy never got anything. I understand the piano was still in the house?" he asked Anton.

"Yes it was, and still is. The new owners have a family and their son wants to learn to play. They were thrilled about it being left there for them. I cleaned and polished it all up, and tuned it in readiness for when they move in. It looks like new now."

"Was that old rocker still in there? I heard the old woman never left it, sat in it all the time while she waited for Billy."

"Yes, it's there alright. I left that too, and the new owners seem intent on keeping it. The husband's going to refurbish it because he's in the manufacturing upholstery business."

"Ah well, at least it's finally got a good home." He carried on with his story: "Billy passed away you know, not long before Old Jim. He's buried in the church graveyard – at least he got that if nothing else. The plot was reserved for Magdalena, but because she was sent to the madhouse by Beryl she didn't get a proper burial and wasn't laid to rest where she was meant to be. I heard she was cremated. Anyway, she'd be happy to know Billy was there and long may they both rest in peace now."

"Is the grave marked?"

"There's no fancy headstone, just a small round stone, very smooth just like a pebble. No-one knows who put it there it just turned up one day. It has nothing on it except a small inscription which reads *Billy*. There wasn't anyone to care about him really, and I doubt if anyone knew he was there. No-one knew him you see cos he'd been gone too long – gone and forgotten. You'll find it down the side of the church, facing the direction of Juniper. It's easy to find anyway because it's the only one with a stone."

The barman finished shining the last of the pint glasses and Anton finished his drink. He put the empty glass on the bar.

"What happened to Beryl?" asked Anton quietly, as an afterthought.

"She went mad and ended up in the same madhouse as her mother. She used to say that her mother was haunting her at Juniper, and had used the cat as a medium to get to her. She got her comeuppance in the end. It wouldn't surprise me if Magdalena met her there, at the madhouse, and carried on haunting her to her death. Serves her right whatever she got."

"I'll be off then and if I can leave these keys here, the couple will be in later this week." Anton slid the keys across to the barman who picked them up and placed them on a hook behind the bar.

Anton made a move to leave but couldn't resist glancing across the bar to the corner where he'd first seen Billy. A great sadness clung heavily to his shoulders, as he reflected on the tragic story the landlord had relayed to him. But as he was about to walk away, he was taken by surprise as he saw the old man looking across at him from his usual corner. Anton instinctively lifted his hand to wave, and then stopped dead in his tracks. He didn't know if it was a figment of his imagination, or whether he was truly seeing him. The old man lifted his half-empty glass of beer and smiled across to Anton, nodding to him at the same time. Anton made a move to walk round to him but the old man disappeared within seconds, leaving Anton to wonder if it had really happened.

He was visibly shaken, but he finally realised that Billy was thanking him for all what he'd done by his efforts at bringing a lifelong mystery to a close. If he hadn't been somehow led to the house to buy and renovate it, the secret may have remained a mystery for many more years to come, and maybe forever. And the ghosts that lived within it would have remained there unable to rest in peace. He had been responsible, along with Lucy, for uncovering an age-long crime. When Billy made the decision to give him the keys that day, he must have decided it was time.

But the crime should have been solved all those years ago, so that the perpetrators could have been caught and punished. Billy could have been reunited with his doting mother and therefore have given a very sad story a happy ending. At the same time, Beryl might never have been able to subject her mother to the cruelty and treachery bestowed upon her by her only daughter. But for whatever reason, it hadn't to be. There was no turning back of events, things happen for a reason, but that was for someone else to justify, Anton certainly couldn't.

He decided to walk up the lane to take a look at the graveyard to see if he could find Billy's resting place and to pay his respects, albeit years too late. He opened the small latch gate which struggled and groaned as he pushed it, probably due to lack of use. He wandered round to the side of the church, the side overlooking Juniper, and there it was in a corner. Just as the landlord had said, a small stone marked Billy's grave.

He stood and reflected for a while. All of the past months' events were beyond his understanding and he may never be able to work it out. But he'd grown fond of the old man – or fond of his memory whichever was most appropriate. Because he knew now that when he first set eyes on Billy he had somehow managed to slip into a time-warp with him, which allowed him to experience a glimpse into the past. He was unlikely to ever work out how he obtained the keys from someone who was buried in the earth just below his feet; but some unknown force far beyond the reach of human comprehension, had somehow lured him into a situation for which he was destined. And who was he to question a higher intelligence than his own.

He walked away after saying a quiet goodbye to Billy, but part way down the lane something compelled him to look back. In the distance he saw the shadowy outline of a woman kneeling at the grave. She seemed to look up and wave to him, and then she was gone. He turned away and kept on walking, convinced his eyes had deceived him and he cast it out of his mind.

As he strolled back down the lane, the rain came on and the skies took on a grey hue. He clutched at his Granddad's old cardie which he was wearing, and pulled it tightly round his body to keep him warm whilst he made his way to the pub car park and his old camper van.

He knew he wouldn't be passing through Judge Fields again, unless one day they decided to take that old top road to their favourite village after all; who knows. Right now he had no plans to return.

He cast his mind back to Billy, and the shadowy image at his graveside, but he had no knowledge or understanding of these things. They had always intended to walk round the old graveyard and browse through the ancient headstones, but somehow the opportunity had never arisen. And all the times that he had looked for signs of the pub opening, so that he could call in and speak to the old man once more, little did he know, or even guess, that his name was Billy and he was lying in the church graveyard, a smooth round stone marking his grave and pointing in the direction of Juniper. Maybe, after all, the shadowy image at the graveside could be that of his mother, Magdalena. He would never know of course, and better to leave the past alone and cast his mind to the future.

His long stride soon turned into a run as he hurried back to the shelter of his old camper van and jumped in out of the rain. He took one last look at the old pub and then drove away out of the car park, out of the hamlet of Judge Fields, and onto the main road which would take him back home to where he belonged with Lucy.

Peppi Hilton

Epilogue

At the graveside
The earth grows rich above your face the flowers bloom each year
And down within that earth-filled space you are so still my dear
So many words were left unsaid so many things undone
So many thoughts within my head were meant for you alone
And as my tears refresh the soil that covers you whilst you sleep
My last sweet words *I love you* are yours alone to keep.

The end

Peppi Hilton

Author's Note:

Thank you for choosing to purchase this book, I hope you enjoyed reading it.

Amazon offers all of their customers the opportunity to post a review on their site, so that the reader can give their opinion on a book, whether good or bad. I would like to ask if you could find the time to post your review of this book on Amazon, as it would be greatly appreciated. Reviews can only act to improve an author's work, and to be given an insight into a reader's thoughts is extremely valuable. Purchasing a book does not guarantee that a reader has enjoyed. Your feedback is very precious. Please give your view if you can.

If you have enjoyed this book, you may also wish to take a look at 'The Appointment', which is now available on Amazon as a kindle version and paperback.

To keep up to date with new releases, visit my website and blog at: peppihilton.co.uk where you can also leave your comments if you wish.

Thank you,

Sincerely yours,

Peppi Hilton

Printed in Great Britain
by Amazon